The West Is the Light
Volume One: Heed the Call

Eddie Zapata

Aristos Books—Louisville, CO
Paperback ISBN: 979-8-218-37361-0
Hardcover ISBN: 979-8-218-34946-2
Library of Congress Control Number: 2023924440
Title: *The West Is the Light: Volume One: Heed the Call*
Author: Eddie Zapata
Digital distribution | 2023
Paperback | 2023

Illustrated by Junior's Digital Design

This is a work of fiction. The characters, names, incidents, places, and dialogue are products of the author's imagination, and are not to be construed as real.

Dedication

To my beautiful mother, Delia, who made everything possible.

Introduction

I believe that the West is dying, and I want to help it recover, as I would want to help a beloved parent who is dying. The following pages are my attempt to restore our dying parent to health. In them, you will find a passion for making the children of the West love their ailing parent again. For the children of the West have contracted an illness, and they have gone mad, and now prick their parent with thousands of small wounds, bleeding her to death.

Book One

If we could dredge up something forgotten not only by ourselves but by our whole generation or our entire civilization, we should become indeed the boonbringer, the culture hero of the day—a personage of not only local but world historical moment.
— Joseph Campbell, <u>The Hero With a Thousand Faces</u>

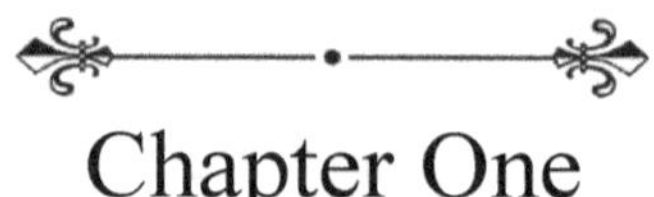

Chapter One

A boy of twelve years sits on his bed with a beautiful book on his lap. His name is Clark. It is raining outside. He gazes for some moments at the droplets as they streak down the window. He feels the cold coming in from the gray through his window, but he also feels the warmth of the blankets around his body. He feels safe and relishes the feeling. In this comfortable state, he reads the large hardbound tome. It is a gift from his grandfather, who has traveled the world. Oversized and with a glossy cover, the pages are filled with colorful pictures of European artworks and architecture — Greek marble statues, stone cairns, Baroque church facades, ornate French parlors with fireplaces and libraries, and the like. The title is <u>The Light of Western Civilization</u>. The boy is drawn in by the aesthetic of the pictures. The text also tantalizes. Every chapter begins with a large, very stylized first letter, like an illuminated Gospel manuscript from the early medieval period.

His eyes take in all, even the errata at the beginning, telling of publication date and edition number. He feels that the book is a sanctuary from a chaotic world. Here he will read of inventors, explorers, artists, poets, knights, wars, treaties, invasions, plagues, lovers, saints and mystics. Through it all, he senses an indescribable longing, as of a long-lost relative who loved him but who has been forgotten.

The boy does not see an invisible young female form next to him, gently stroking his soft, wavy light brown hair and cooing over him, smiling tenderly.

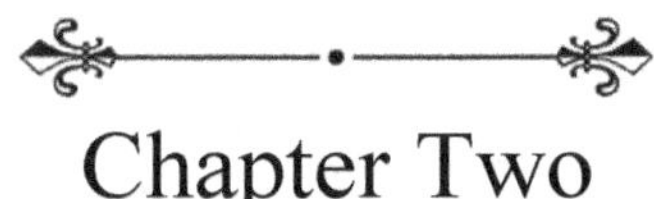

Chapter Two

Dear reader, I want you to know that the people you will meet in this story have all come out of the book Clark is reading. Although they do not know it, now you do. Eventually Clark will meet them all, even though some will not appear in his life until he is an adult. All of them, the men, the women, the children, the old people, have also been visited by the pretty young woman who now sits next to Clark. We shall soon meet them.

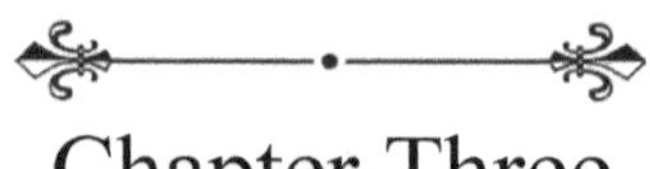

Chapter Three

"**I** want to travel the world like my grandfather when I get older," Clark thinks.

He has always been a different sort of boy, different from boys his own age. From as early as he can remember, his imagination has been as active as a volcano in full fury. Images, scenarios, conversations, re-configurations of the people and situations around him came to him as easily as breathing. He could sit alone in his room, or patiently wait as his parents shopped in stores, perfectly amused within the mansions of his mind. He did not crave the activities natural to other children; in fact, felt hindered by them, as failing to satisfy the higher order of joy afforded by his inner eye. His imagination was like a friend that never left him, and always wanted to play the most absorbing and original games conceivable.

When Clark discovered reading, his imagination soared even higher upon newly discovered wings, revealing greater and more astonishing vistas to an already inebriated intelligence. His mental activity, like a small rivulet, joined with the larger, more energetic streams and rivers flowing from myriad writers, and gained momentum. As his powers of interior creation waxed, so did his vocabulary. He would both profit and chafe as a result of this transformation. Gifted children wield a double edged sword that does not spare them.

His eyes get big as he scans the pictures. As he flips the pages, he pauses and wonders at what he sees: Leonardo da Vinci's peculiar *Vitruvian Man;* the white, lacy ceiling of the Divinity School at Oxford; a muscular bison swelling forth from the ceiling of a cave in Spain; the Temple of Concordia in Sicily; an oil painting by someone named Jan van Eyck titled *The Ghent Altarpiece;* a heavy-looking medieval German longsword, and many other images of the European patrimony. Clark imagines himself entering each photograph and becoming friends with the people of those lands and times. A photo of the castle at Carcassonne in France immediately transports him to its ramparts, dressed for battle in his suit of armor, discussing strategy with his fellow knights. Another photo, of the interior of a medieval church bathed in a soft golden candlelight, the altar prepared for the sacrifice, evokes a piety that surprises Clark. "Why do I feel connected to these places?" he ponders in his heart.

He flips the pages and occasionally stops to read some of the text. One chapter deals with knighthood and chivalry. A mounted knight stares out at the reader. He wears a colorful heraldic device on his armor, a roaring creature of deep scarlet, possibly a dragon, but Clark isn't sure. It rears on its haunches on a field of gold, bordered by black weapons. Beside the warrior is a quote: *"Think again, of knights and ladies, of the court and field, that bonded us in love and courtesy."* The quote is from someone named Dante, an Italian who wrote a book called <u>The Divine Comedy</u>. "The *Divine* Comedy? How can something holy be funny also?" He makes a mental note to investigate this fellow Dante and his book later.

Although Clark begins feeling drowsy, he stubbornly continues perusing the pages, hungry for new stimulations. His eyes begin to droop, even as he tries pronouncing some of the foreign words and phrases, whose unfamiliarity provokes wonder and a thirst for translation: γνῶθι σεαυτόν (gnothi seuton); in hoc signo vinces; Gott mit uns; Éire go Brách, and others. On one page is a fancy flower called a fleur-de-lys next to a lovely girl with a serious look on her face. The girl is someone he has heard of, but knows little of—Joan of Arc. Above her head are the words, "Messire Dieu, premier servi." He concentrates on the words, trying his best to translate them into English without looking at the provided translations, but the effort makes him drowsy, and he dozes off.

The pretty dark-haired girl next to him gently closes the book.

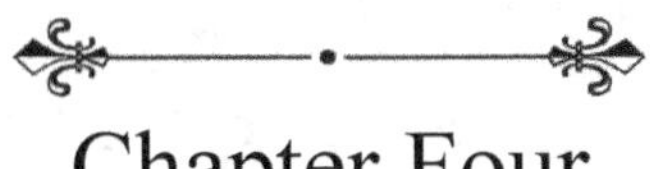

Chapter Four

When Clark opens his eyes, there is a kindly man smiling at him. He wears a plaid flat cap and a thick tweed coat. Wisps of salt and pepper hair emerge from under his cap by his ears. Brown corduroy trousers descend to well-worn, brown shoes, like workmen's shoes, with blades of grass attached by moisture to the soles. Cold emanates from his clothes, as if he has suddenly walked in from a wintry day, bringing some of it with him. He appears in his fifties or sixties. He has a fleshy nose, a broad forehead, sparkling eyes, and the smile of a man visiting a beloved relation he has not seen in a long time. He is portly without being obese, and exudes an easy, cordial confidence. Boy and man stare at each other for a moment, Clark's mouth open, marveling.

The smiling man says, "Well hello there Clark! And how are you today?" His voice is rich and honeyed and sounds like home and safety. He has an accent that Clark has heard somewhere before, maybe in a movie, but he can't identify it.

"Uh, uh, I'm doing ok," he finally manages to stammer.

"Ha ha! That's good to hear, my fine young lad. I know this is strange for you, my being here, but I don't want you to be frightened. I have come a long way and I want to introduce you to some people and places that I know you're going to enjoy. Your grandfather, who cares about you very much, wants me to show you these things, since he can't himself, being so far away at the moment. Would you like to travel to the places in that book you have there and meet those people and get to know them and their ways?"

This is precisely what Clark wants most, and he begins to smile in response to the offer. "Yes, but how can I? I'm not old enough to go by myself."

The man laughs good-naturedly and answers, "We're not going to travel the usual way. We're going to use that book," here he points at Clark's gift from his grandfather, "as a vehicle of transportation. But I haven't introduced myself yet. I apologize. Let me ask you first," his

eyes twinkle with youthful mirth as he cocks his head, "can you tell where I'm from by my way of speaking?" The way he said the words sounded like, *can yee tell weere ahm from by mee way o' speekin.*

Clark thinks about it, but he is too proud to guess incorrectly, so he meekly offers, "Um, somewhere like, around England?" Clark suspects that the man might not actually be English, and might even take offense at his guess, although Clark wouldn't be able to answer why. He simply has an instinct about the way other people feel.

The man replies, "Close to England, yes, but north. Do you know what country is north of England? It's alright if you don't. No? I'm from Scotland, and my name is Alistair.

"Now, if we're going to be traveling together, we might want to get better acquainted. So what do you say we sit and chat for a while before embarking on our journey? You can ask me whatever you'd like and I promise to tell the truth, unless I'm really, really embarrassed by it." Here he gives out a cavernous laugh that infects Clark as well. After chuckling, Alistair continues, "And I would like to ask you some questions too, if I may."

"Sure, that would be ok." Clark's initial bafflement is giving way to thrill.

"Well, would you like to go first?" Alistair asks.

I would, Clark thinks, but I'm so overwhelmed by events that I can't think straight. He says to Alistair, "No that's ok, you can go first."

Alistair nods, and asks, "What do you like about that book that your grandfather gave you?"

"Um, well, it's just so full of beautiful places and people, that it makes me want to jump inside of it and see that world for myself. And also, I don't know why, but I feel like there's something familiar about it. Like I'm looking at stuff that is a part of me, but that I'm separate from. I don't know, it's hard to explain."

Alistair has been listening intently, leaning slightly forward. "I think you did a fine job of explaining. Yes, I understand you, young Clark. The reason why you feel that way is because you ARE connected to those people and places, and in more ways than one. But you see, you're an American, and you were born far away, both in time and space, from the people and places in the book, so you feel disconnected. But there is something inside of you that remembers." He gestures with his finger pointing at Clark's torso. "Your blood. You are connected to those people by blood, and when your eyes look at pictures of knights in armor, or Spartan warriors with spears in hand, or the ceiling of that chapel in Italy painted by the great Michelangelo, your blood reacts. It knows. It tries to whisper to your mind, but your mind doesn't always understand, because it's not used to thinking like that. The blood thinks one way, the mind another."

This answer satisfies Clark deeply. *Here is someone who gets me,* he thinks. Clark has longed to express the yearnings that had begun surging from an unexpected spring in his soul, but at his age his vocabulary fails him, even though he is advanced for a twelve-year old. Besides, his friends at school seem to lack the sensitivity he has recently developed. They are out of harmony with his mind and its delights. Whenever he tries broaching certain subjects, they seem indifferent. Once or twice he was jeered. So he learned to keep his mouth shut, but silently nurses a desire to find his own kind, a society proportioned to him who understands him profoundly and responds to his soul-stirrings. Clark somehow senses their presence in the wider world, but remains helplessly ignorant as how to contact them. Could Alistair be one of these separated brethren?

Moved thusly, Clark spontaneously asks Alistair, "Do YOU ever feel like that? Like you're disconnected from your people? I mean, I know you're from over there, but still."

Alistair purses his lips in thought. "Not lately, no, but *once* I did."

Alistair has a tendency of emphasizing certain words, so the word "once" receives a special weight in this case. "Even though I'm from 'over *there*,' as you say," he smiles teasingly at Clark, "Scotland is far away from the continent. Or at least, that's how it felt, being so far north at a time when travel was difficult, and communication slow. We felt sometimes like a *forgotten* people, a people who haven't been *invited* to the party down south, where all the *action* is going on. Ha ha! My peers weren't always keen on what was happening beyond our *borders*, as I was. And so, Clark, there were times when I felt like I lived in a world created inside my *head*, a world that was perfect and beautiful, a world I wanted to *share* with others. But whenever I got to talking about it, people just smiled and turned *away*, or changed the subject. But I still had friends and got on well with others. You see, we can't turn inside *ourselves* and lock ourselves away from others. That's not the *way* of our species. Especially not if you have a lot to share with the world, as I think *you* do, Clark." He winks at Clark, who feels flattered to be highly thought of by one of the most interesting men he has ever met.

"It's tempting, I know, to become very picky about whom you talk to and whom you avoid. Like one of your American poets said, a lady poet it was, 'The soul selects her own society.' Yet there IS a way to love Beauty and not go into exile from the rest of humanity." This last part steadies Clark. Something about Alistair's choice of the word "beauty" echoes in his heart. And why had he said it as if were capitalized?

"Well, my fine lad, now that we're not total strangers anymore, what do you say we begin our travels? Aren't you eager to get going?"

Am I ever, Clark thought. A few doubts and questions occur to him in quick succession, like what to do about food and lodging, but Clark's instincts arise again and he quickly dismisses these doubts. All will be disposed of properly, he feels assured, though uncertain why.

"Yeah, let's do it! Let's go."

Clark leaps up and hurriedly throws together a knapsack with clothes and toiletries.

With a hearty laugh, Alistair picks up the glossy, hardcover book of European culture, and invites Clark to place his hand on its cover. "As soon as you do that, we're off."

Clark's eyes grow large, his mouth opens in wonderment. He stretches out his right hand, places it resolutely on the book cover, looks up into Alistair's eyes, and tries his best to prepare himself for what comes next. As he does so, a third person in the bedroom looks on, smiling her approval, and bestowing her blessing on the boy.

Chapter Five

Clark thought he saw a flash of light, but he is not certain. No, it wasn't a flash of light, it was more like a sudden movement and a blur of colors as the environment around him rushed by. Once the sense of dislocation passes, he looks around. He and Alistair are standing in a grassy field with a wide sky above them. Around them, punctuating the green grass, are very bright white daisies with bright yellow centers. Puffy, billowing clouds adorn the blue field of sky. The ground is not flat, but gradually slopes down. He looks around, trying to take it all in, and eventually his eyes alight upon an object resting upon the field in the distance. Down below him, in a depression, are several very large stones arranged in a circle. His gaze sharpens, and he narrows his eyes. He has seen them before, but can't remember what they are called.

"What are those, Alistair? I've seen them before somewhere."

"Those, my young companion, are the stones of Stonehenge. And we are standing in a location known for a time as Sarum, in the southwest of England. You see, if we're going to introduce you to Europe as the 'light of western civilization,' it's a good idea to start somewhere far in the past, so we can look out over her history as if looking across a field from a height. Just as we are doing now. Go ahead and drink it all in, I won't rush you. We'll start walking down to the stones soon enough."

Clark does look around and does drink it all in. This is his first time traveling, except when his family went to the Grand Canyon, but he was younger then, and doesn't remember much of that trip. So he assents to the wind that strokes his face, he drinks in the springtime earthiness through his nostrils, he turns his body, and looks, and looks, and looks. A peace descends upon him, and he revels in it. This peace is something he has often wished for, when he has knelt in church and admired the glow of stained-glass windows. When he has read tales of far-away castles shrouded in mist. When he has simply lain on his bed and stared at the ceiling, aching because called to a greater experience, but helpless to answer the summons.

Where are the people and the cars and the buildings? he wonders after recovering from his reverie. But he dismisses the thought as unimportant. Better to remain silent, dreamily enchanted with the charm of this idyll.

At some point he finds himself walking down into the lower valley, Alistair at his side, humming a Scottish air that echoes in his powerful, deep chest.

As they draw closer, Clark notices some of the stones wearing patches of green, like moss on trees. The patches confer a fuzziness upon the stones that seems queer. The megaliths also bulge with a girth more noticeable when standing in front of them than when seen in photographs. There are no guard rails or informational stations in sight, but as before, Clark thinks it better not to ask questions.

Standing in front of a slab, facing east, Alistair says to Clark, "Now I want you to listen to me. That book you're holding there, it's more than our transportation. It's also a means of communication. Now that we're standing here in front of Stonehenge, I want you to find the section of your book that deals with this place. Open to it, and let me know when you find it."

Clark dutifully does as he is asked. He consults the table of contents, finds a chapter titled, "Beginnings," and flips to the page indicated. There is a two-page spread showing the very location they are at now, with some text at the top in bold and smaller text at the bottom. Clark was about to tell Alistair he had found it, as he is eager to find out what was meant by "means of communication," when he notices something odd about the picture. There are two individuals standing in front of the cyclopean stones. At first Clark thinks little of it, but as he focuses on them, he realizes with mounting amazement that both he and Alistair are in the book!

"Well, are you there yet?"

"Yeah, but, but..."

"What's the matter Clark?"

"Alistair, look, we're in the book! See? That's us standing in front of Stonehenge, just like we're doing now."

Alistair looks down at the boy with a glowing smile. "And why shouldn't we be in your book, since this is your story, and as I am your traveling companion, I will appear from time to time also."

"My story?"

"Yes, your story. Isn't that what you wished for? To enter the world of the book and meet the people you found there and have adventures? Well here you are, Clark: at the beginning of your story."

Clark weighs the import of all Alistair has said. After a few moments of crinkling his forehead, "You mean, all this is for me? Everything we're going to go through has to do with me?"

"Yes. Remember, I told you your grandfather knows you well, knows the kind of mind you have, and he wants to foster it. But not only your mind and your intelligence, also your character. Because a powerful mind in a person of weak or evil character can be a dangerous thing at worst, an annoying thing at best. And he wants you to be the best version of yourself Clark. And so here we are."

Clark can't help but be touched to hear about his grandfather's concern for him. He promises himself to make some kind of gift, some offering to his grandfather expressing his appreciation for so much care.

Clark has always liked his grandfather. He enjoys hearing his stories about distant lands and strange customs. His grandfather has a way of expressing himself that no other adult has, and he always brings enthusiasm into his descriptions. Clark also can't help but notice that he is his grandfather's favorite grandchild. He thinks this is because his grandfather sees some of himself in Clark. I'll have to ask him if he had dreams of traveling when he was my age, he thinks. And why he is so different from the rest of his family. Maybe I'll understand *myself* better.

"I don't want to disappoint him, and I also want the same. But is there something I have to do while we're in this world, or can I just look around? I mean, I feel like there is a test I have to pass at some point. I'm not sure why I feel this way, I just do."

A look of mild concern briefly appears on Alistair's face then quickly goes away. He regains his cheerful demeanor almost at once.

"We'll take things one step at a time, Mr. Clark, and if we come to something that needs dealing with in a certain manner, we'll deal with it then. Now, shall we get to know the story of these big, thick stones a bit better?"

"Ok, but what did you mean when you said the book is a means of communication?"

"We're arriving at that. You see, that book is a special thing. It looks like something you'd find in any bookstore, but that's only a disguise, a kind of camouflage, if you will. It's real origin and purpose are quite unique, known only to a few, such as your grandfather. But to get back to your question.

"The book responds only to a *true* question. By that I mean, it will only answer a question that you have adequately pondered and that comes from an honest yearning. Do not ask frivolous, half-hearted questions. Not that you are the frivolous type, but sometimes we get reckless or lazy.

"So what I want you to do now is consider the stones in front of you. Allow a question to form in your mind. It should come from a pure part of your mind, with no nonsense attached to it. You will know when it is pure. Usually it comes to you within seconds, occasionally it takes a while longer to formulate.

"Once the question takes shape in your head, and you can see it with your inner eye, then you ask it of the book. You must be in the section of the book that's associated with your question, and you have to place your right hand on the book like when we use it for travel. Then, facing the person or the object or the place that your question involves, you ask it by barely moving your lips, like you're whispering a secret to someone, or murmuring a prayer.

"After you do that, just wait. You will receive your answer in one of two ways: internally or externally. By internally I mean it will be an answer inside your mind. By externally I mean you will see or hear something or someone who serves as a reply. Sometimes the reply is obvious, sometimes it is veiled, and you have to meditate on it, search out its meaning."

Clark's head is swimming with the implications of all Alistair has said. What he has just heard serves to confirm that this adventure IS specially suited for him. How many times has Clark felt his heart stirred by unquenched longing when he read a moving description of a brave warrior on the cusp of resisting a dragon, or a weary, bedraggled party just discovering a lost temple in a deep jungle? Here now is a means to unfetter his heart and sling it towards its object of desire instead of sharing in its disconsolateness.

With this new dawn breaking in his breast he turns towards the megaliths of Stonehenge. With book in hand, he regards the ancient craftwork. He opens pathways of thought and desire. His natural wistfulness now serves his purpose. His breathing becomes shallow. He stops blinking. Lively anticipation yields to disciplined imagination. Quietened and tractable, he murmurs, "What were the longings of the people that constructed you, what compelled them to will you into existence, so vast in the depths of your mystery?"

There follows a pregnant void, which slowly turns into a shimmering, a vibration. Golden light beams flutter like curtains in a breeze around the edges of Clark's field of vision. He cannot vouchsafe if they are truly visible or not. Everything appears to bulge as if the canvas of an oil painting were being stretched from behind by an ox's massive head.

Out of this prodigy blooms an answer to Clark's question, like a voluptuous efflorescing of a tender green bud. He cannot maintain whether he hears the response with his ears, or within his mind, or otherwise, but it matters not. The act is completed, his satisfaction unassailable.

Chapter Six

For some moments Clark wobbles there, supported by rapture. Gradually the feeling diminishes and his breathing deepens, his lips slightly parted in awe. He sends a wordless "thank you" to he knows not whom.

From afar he faintly hears his name until he recovers enough to realize Alistair is speaking to him.

"Clark? How was it? How was your first experience with The Joining?"

"Alistair, I can hardly talk right now. I'm sorry."

The man grins broadly and laughs warmly. "It's alright. We don't have to speak. We can just enjoy a bit of quiet if you'd like."

"No, I actually DO want to talk about it, I just need a second to recover."

After a few deep breaths, Clark continues. "That was one of the most beautiful things that's ever happened to me. I could almost cry, but I don't want to be a baby. But why did you call it The Joining?"

"That's just the name we've assigned to the rare gift bestowed by your special book. We *join* with an aspect of creation more deeply and meaningfully than usual when we consult the oracle." Here Alistair indicates the book. "It seems to fit the experience, don't you think?"

"Alistair, why was I chosen for this?"

Clark asks the question with a ripening surmise. He half anticipates what Alistair will say.

"You were chosen because you, and other young boys and girls like you, belong to a certain class of people. I won't go into greater detail than that for now, because you are not yet at that stage of the journey. Don't try to encompass the whole riddle yet. You are in training. Focus on the lessons, and trust that you will be brought into full knowledge when the time is ripe."

Alistair's way of speaking appeals to Clark. He has always felt more adult-like than his peers, and he enjoys developing his powers of intellect and vocabulary. But he suffers the frustration of isolation.

Circumstances have denied him fellowship with coequals. Now with Alistair, he feels mollified and also challenged to excel.

"Should I tell you what the stones told me?" Some inner urging compels Clark to frame the question thusly.

"Not unless you want to. It's never required to share what the book reveals. Those are personal matters, meant only for the chambers of your heart."

Alistair then does something that inexplicably comforts Clark. He reaches into an inner pocket of his jacket and produces a pipe. He then removes some tobacco from what looks like waxed paper and very contentedly commences to smoke.

From the corner of his eye the man espies the boy watching him. He asks in a playfully serious tone, "You're not thinking about taking a puff of my tobacco, are ye?"

"Well to tell you the truth…"

"Avast, ye saucy whelp! You'll have to wait 'til you're older."

Both enjoy a good laugh.

Chapter Seven

Two days have passed since Stonehenge. Boy and man have enjoyed talks, walks, and repasts under an unvaryingly serene sky and amidst gentle breezes. Clark has learned that when mealtime arrives, Alistair leads his young ward in a certain direction known only to him and the pair come across a picnic spread in a cozy spot. This curiosity, like others before it, also occasioned a prompting to remain silent, but Clark permitted himself an exception.

"So do you feel like telling me how you know where to find food and stuff?"

"Let's just say it's an ability you acquire when you've been part of my club for a while."

"Alistair, when you said I belonged to a certain class of people…"

"Yes?"

"Are you a part of that class too?"

"Yes. I was called when I was younger, about your age. I was recruited, you might say. A choice was placed before me, and I made a decision."

"Is my path going to be the same as yours?"

"How do you mean?"

"I mean, well I guess, …"

"If you mean whether you will encounter the same challenges as me, find yourself in the same situations as me, then no, probably not. Our paths will be different just like the lives of any two individuals are different. But if you mean 'walk the same path' in a general sort of way, well, I suppose all of us share certain commonalities. For instance, we all are called upon to live honorably and responsibly. But, as I said before, now is not the time for an abundance of details. For now, I merely wish you to take in this adventure, as if you were breathing in the air of a mountain village you are visiting for the first time, and find out if it suits you or not."

The pair have arrived at their lunch during their talk and now are sitting down to take their tea. Clark has been introduced to the concept of "taking tea" courtesy of Alistair, who is as civilized a man as one could hope for. He admitted that the only tea he had ever drank was iced tea, and Alistair taught him the art of preparing a perfect cup of the delicious liquid.

They now dig into a wicker basket full of fragrant scones and proceed to lather butter and jam all over the airy pastries. This too is a novelty for Clark. His first bite into one of these softly yielding delicacies ensured a lifelong devotion. The combination of buttery, jam-slathered scone with a hot cup of silky, creamy tea with sugar converted him into a European on the spot.

There were also sausages cooked in oil and butter on a small portable stove which Alistair took command of. The crackle of the meat and the sizzle of the juices joined with the savory smell to make Clark's mouth water whenever they cooked. Over-medium eggs seasoned with salt and pepper rounded the picture; yolks not too runny, not too hard, but with the consistency of thick honey in a cool jar.

At night there were the stars. Clark is from a crowded American city which had banished the night sky decades ago, and so had rarely seen the Milky Way or the constellations. He receives from Alistair an astronomical education. He learns to identify the pageantry of mythology woven into the blackness of space. He further learns to distinguish planets from stars. He revels in his first meteor shower, which elicits a wide-eyed "whoa" from him. The night sky gingerly disrobes and reveals its subtleties of colors to Clark's eager eyes, as he scans the heavens from quadrant to quadrant in thankfulness and absorption. Sleep comes upon him many times in this state.

Clark's thoughts upon the threshold of sleep return to what the stones had said. He could not describe in words exactly how he learned the answer to his question, because it seemed to formulate itself outside of the normal channels of communication. He did not so much "hear" or "see" anything as such, but it was as if someone else were thinking for him, and he was both himself and not himself in that moment. And yet certain images did form in his mind during this strange exchange. Somehow, he sensed a young boy about his own age standing in a circle of mostly adults. The circle wrapped around Stonehenge. They were gathered in order to celebrate the completion of its latest embellishment and for its rededication. It was nighttime, and torches cast dancing black shadows on the recently worked stones. The boy wore an animal skin tunic and a necklace of shells and bones. Around his waist was fastened a belt with a rudimentary knife. Clark somehow knew that the boy's knife would be traded for a larger, sharper tool once he became a man. Beyond the circle of light cast by the boy's tribe was a vast and foreboding forest, a forest now vanished. Three or four men stood in front of the monument, speaking loudly to be heard by all. Their audience kept a respectful silence. The men spoke of the debt their people owed their gods. The people must show gratitude and awe to their gods for success in the hunt, the protection of their women in childbirth, the raising of healthy children, and shelter from calamities such as violent storms and plague.

The men ceased speaking and all was quiet for a long moment. Then all present seemed to freeze, temporarily turned into lifeless and soulless mannequins. An event of great moment was about to break forth which required stillness. Next, Clark apprehended that from somewhere beyond the scene he was witnessing, or perhaps from the direction of the stones, a stream of energy began towards him. It had no form, but to aid Clark's understanding, it dimly assumed the shape of a glowing golden light, such as he saw directly after posing his question. This column of golden light broke just in front of him, as if striking an invisible stone and scattered like a wave. Clark received his message in this manner, and the light seemed to speak to him without audible words, "From age to age we go, and the blood binds us and reminds us and guides us. You are here and they are here in you and through you the next generations live, like the sap in a tree that ever renews itself, ever circulating and vivifying. All you need to know arises from the interplay of your blood with the speech of the Earth, and so will your line continue, healthy and straight, like the flight of an eagle, so long as you heed the call. Do not go to the left or right, do not go crooked, but heed the call. Be prepared to fight and die if necessary, yet always heed the call, heed the call..."

The vision ended in a sudden flare of golden light which abruptly became perfect blackness. Next, Clark was back in the peaceful, sunny, green field next to Alistair. Clark ponders all this over the ensuing days and nights. A part of him understood it instantly, but the full meaning then retreated to a part of his mind that was cloaked from his everyday thinking, like a treasure hidden in a cave by a landslide blocking the entrance. And so Clark spends much of the next few days hewing the rock that separates him from full comprehension. It is a taxing but rewarding labor. It feels like honest, hard work. It feels like heeding the call.

Chapter Eight

Alistair periodically takes his leave of Clark and wanders off just far enough to be out of sight and hearing. He explained it thus to Clark, "My boy, there are times when I will leave you for a brief span of time. I need these moments to *pray*, you might say. Don't fret, I'll only be gone no longer than an hour, and I'm not planning on hopping an airplane and *leaving* you here all by yourself. Old Alistair just needs alone time to clear his head and make sure I'm on the right *path*, is all."

Then Alistair makes for a copse of trees or a swell in the land over which he disappears. Clark shrugs and takes it in stride as part of the wonderfully idiosyncratic nature of his mentor. Besides, it gives him time to explore the fields and woodlands, a pleasure he does not get to enjoy in his city lifestyle.

Alistair walks until he is certain of ensuring he is alone and private. Then he stands still, lets his eyelids droop to a semi-closed position, and interiorly requests an audience with someone. After a brief pause, that someone appears. She is a young, dark-haired beauty, the one who sat by Clark in his bedroom. Upon appearing, the two cordially greet one another and review recent events.

"Hi Alistair. How goes the training of our young page?"

The young woman stands about five feet, five inches. She has hair of raven darkness, healthy and shiny. It is nearly always tied up in a ponytail and bound with a narrow white, silky band. Two delicate coils of dark hair descend from her temples and frame her face. The hair above her forehead lounges in a tuft created from parting her hair on the left side. Her eyes are dark with an undying spark of light in them. Her nose is small and well-formed, like a small acorn. Her ears are also small and neatly folded back, as if held in place by baby angels tugging on them. Her neck is smooth and strong, a tower rising out of her torso. If she were to cast her shadow against a bright white wall of alabaster, she would cast a silhouette as of a woman on a cameo pendant.

Her skin tone ranges between fair and olive, as if just barely bronzed by the sun. No blemish mars her skin or frame, as if such a thing were forbidden by the mandates of Beauty. She habitually wears a form-fitting black dress, which, if seen by one of our world, might be described as a Coco Chanel. Her legs are bare under the hem of the fabric, and they are firm and athletic. The overall impression is of a healthy maiden who has engaged in physical activity from her childhood.

"Good morning Sophie! It's always a pleasure to see you. Oh, it's going fine. Our young friend shows promise thus far of making an addition to the Family."

The pretty girl smiles at this. Indeed, she is nearly always smiling. Her smile seems to emanate from a radiance of light and love in her, an inexhaustible fount of loving-kindness. With one hand on her hip in a pose of youthful femininity, she continues, "That's good to hear, Alistair, good to hear. I knew there was something special about the boy when I first met him. I liked him right away, just like I liked YOU right away." She can't help letting out a soft laugh both at her recollection and of the blush it elicits from Alistair. She laughs with her whole body. Sophia has a tendency to twist at the hips ever so slightly as she speaks, completing the portrait of agreeable maidenhood.

"Alistair, are you almost done with this chapter's lessons? Will you be going to your next engagement soon? It's alright if you need more time; there's no rush. I only ask so I can arrange my schedule better."

"We travel tomorrow; I had already decided. I think Clark is also eager to live more of his adventure. He's taking to it like a fish to water, Sophie. You really know how to pick them."

Laughter. "I'm blessed to hold the commission I do. All my charges give me more than I give them, I'm sure."

"Oh, I wouldn't be too certain about that; but anyway, I think we're all blessed to have found one another."

"Clark asked about being tested. Do you know where his mind is on this matter?"

"No, but I didn't press the issue, but it might subside as we travel along. I'll make sure he has a full plate in front of him so as to keep his mind occupied and off of other matters."

"I'm sure you will Alistair." The pretty girl bestows one of her ample, sweet smiles on the man in the tweed jacket and flat cap and, as always, she draws a like response from him.

Sophia then agilely leans in and gets on her tiptoes to plant a peck on Alistair's cheek. She is fond of chaste kisses on the cheek and confers them on as many people who are not put off by kissing. She seems innately sensitive as to who is receptive. For these, a gentle embrace and kiss from Sophia is as delightful as the return of spring.

"I'll be watching from above and holding you in my heart as always. Call on me if you need me."

Alistair, his heart brimming, pivots and walks away back to Clark. According to custom, he does not look back. It is improper willfully to mark Sophia's appearances and disappearances.

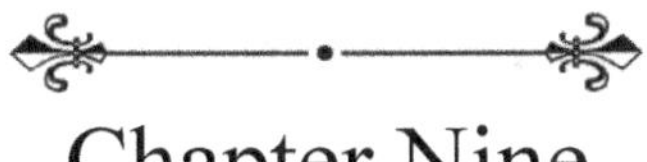

Chapter Nine

Clark's interest in his book, <u>The Light of Western Civilization,</u> has increased greatly. After his initial astonishment subsides enough to allow clarity to return, he returns to it with keen consideration. When he isn't exploring and immersing himself in nature, he reads. He reread the introduction, which offers an overview of Europe from a geological standpoint as well as cultural, and also reads the first chapter, already mentioned, dealing with some of the earliest bright sparks of civilization.

Several selections make an impression on him and linger in his mind after closing the cover of the book. From the Introduction:

While all human civilizations possess some of the attributes listed above said to comprise a civilization, it cannot be ignored that certain peoples attain a level of manifest preeminence in some or all these attributes that is contested only by the most stubborn cynic. The astonishing grandeur of the pyramids along with a flowering of the arts in Egypt; the unity of purpose and refinement of the Chinese; the poetry, horsemanship, and organization of the Persians; the subtlety of philosophical and psychological investigations of India; these and other examples of brilliance attest to the inherent inequality of the human species. Circumstances of physical environment, weather patterns, peculiarities of beliefs, and mere chance conspire along with other factors to produce such prodigies. This book is the chronicle of one such people's journey through time and the manifold fluctuations undergone by them. The European saga is not one of uninterrupted ascent; rather, it is one of fits and starts, of progression and regression, of knowledge lost and knowledge regained. And yet in spite of this flux, perhaps partly due to it, Europe was established on a path towards unparalleled distinction. This work seeks not only to record the events of this trajectory, but to offer insights as to why the European was selected for it.

The chapter titled "Beginnings" offers the following:

Identifying the origin of Western Civilization presents a problem: which Western Civilization are we considering? If we mean only or primarily that culture built upon Greek and Roman foundations, we might ease our task by means of focusing our aim, but there is something fraudulent about starting there. By the time the first Greek epics were written down, a discernible European identity already obtained on most of the continent. We cannot ignore this larger albeit looser kinship. To do so would be to disregard the roots that germinated into that untidy though lush garden we refer to as Europeans. Let us then project ourselves backwards across the millennia and try to arrive at a more common lineage.

These passages set Clark's mind soaring. He pauses and considers his own heritage. His parents rarely raised the matter, except to mention that on his father's side he was mostly English with a touch of Scottish, and on his mother's side Norwegian, French, with maybe some Dutch. This diffusion of bloodlines had somewhat diminished his desire to know more, as there were too many trails to follow. But now he considers his family history with a reinvigorated interest. He develops a sudden yearning to look into the past and see his relatives. What were they like? Did he physically resemble any of them? Would he recognize any of his character traits or those of his living family members in his ancestors? And perhaps most importantly, was there an aggregate wisdom of his line that he might enjoy, as a kind of inheritance? A longing to meet them and talk with them and share his dreams and heart with them overcame Clark. Why have I never given them a thought before? he asks himself. Suddenly his adventure with Alistair takes on an added meaning: he will not only seek to grow as an individual, but he will also seek union with his blood.

Alistair comes along just then whistling a happy tune and preparing his pipe for smoking. He spots Clark with the book in his lap, reclining against a tree. He walks out of the sunlight and into the tree's shade.

"Hello again."

"Hi Alistair." Excitedly he commences, "Hey Alistair, is there a way I can meet my ancestors on this trip?"

Alistair's eyebrows rise a bit at this question. "Hmm. What's behind this request?"

"I've been reading in the book, and some of what I read got me thinking. Like, who am I really? Where do I come from? Why do I act the way I do? Why do I think the way I do? It's weird. I never really thought about this stuff before, but now it's important to me. I want to meet my family, I mean, my historical family and see what they're like. Maybe I can learn something from them, I dunno."

Alistair stands pensive for some moments, regarding the boy. He has lit his pipe and is dispatching blue smoke into the air.

"I'm glad to see your blood awakening to the call of its ancestors. This is a sign I was waiting for. You've arrived at it sooner than the others."

"Others?"

"My other pupils. I've been doing this for a while. And you are the first student to ask about his predecessors within the first few days. Yes, Clark, we can meet them. But not right away. We need to see more and learn more, get the lay of the land, as it were. Then we can steer a path that leads to your kin. And that, my young friend, is always a delight."

Clark grins mightily. He is inebriated with novelty and expectancy. There follows a vigorous questioning of Alistair concerning his own family line. Clark has become a genealogist of a sudden and pursues his métier with a passion. Alistair is game, and seems to enjoy answering. Clark marvels at the man's descriptions of family crests, tartans of various patterns, warrior codes, pioneers who left for the continent, rakes who seduced the womenfolk; a whole gallery of individuals that embodies the multiplicity of human temperaments.

"Alistair, I'm even more grateful than before that you came for me and brought me into this experience. I can't wait for the next day!"

"I hope every day finds you so ardent. Now let's get some rest, because tomorrow we ride again."

The pair settles in according to their manner: Alistair with his pipe, Clark with his book. And so they remained until nightfall.

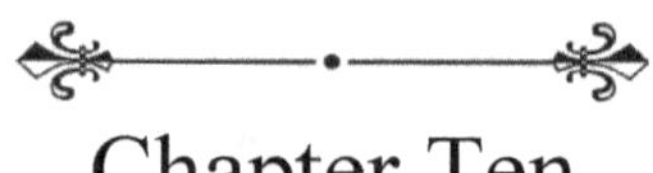

Chapter Ten

The next morning the pair sit down to another satisfying breakfast. Clark asks if he can help, and is placed in charge of cooking rashers of bacon. He prepares them on the chewy side rather than crispy, his favorite.

Alistair then asks Clark a curious question: "Clark, what are your thoughts on hard physical activity, like surviving in the woods, working with your hands, and on fighting?"

"Well I mean, I've had it pretty easy I guess. I don't have to do a lot of really hard work."

"Ha ha, yes, you seem to live in a post-labor age. But if you *had* to?"

"I want to learn that stuff. I mean, I feel like every guy should know how to handle himself. Because if you don't, I feel like then you're not really a man, you know? And I want to become the strongest, most confident man I can be. So yeah, I don't mind learning all that stuff: how to survive in the wild, start fires, hunt, fish, and fight too." Alistair does not answer, but gives Clark an approving nod. Clark wants to ask more, but again his impulse is to wait until Alistair chooses to tell him more.

The two clean up and arrange their belongings. A nearby stream of clean, sparkling water has provided their drinking and bathing necessities, and the two avail themselves of it this morning as usual. Then, Alistair summons his ward to extend his hand as before and place it upon the book. Clark does so, there is an expectancy, and then a blur, and then they are elsewhere and elsewhen.

*　　*　　*

They rematerialize in front of a cave. Around them are a few medium-sized trees, and scrubby vegetation. Jagged rocks lie strewn about the front of the cave's opening, and long, thorny stalks of wild grass sway in the wind. This time, Clark has some idea what awaits him. He has read further in his book, and learned of a cave in Spain with remarkable paintings on the walls done by prehistoric human beings. The colors are so vibrant, and the artistic merit so high, that Clark can hardly credit such a feat was accomplished by people living thousands of years ago. "Just how far back does the idea of Beauty go?" he ponders.

Alistair leads the two into the cave. After ducking their heads and scrambling over some scree, they arrive at the inner cathedral. The cave is dark, but Alistair produces a light from his deep pockets. It is powerful, and illuminates a wide swath of the cave. Outside the lamplight is a deep darkness that borders the drawings like the frame of an oil painting.

Clark gazes at the artwork, mouth agape, for long moments. Animals of an older world run and twist their sinewy bodies. Some are solitary, some run in herds. The images seem as if they had been prancing just a heartbeat ago and then suddenly froze. They might move again any moment. Their colors of brown, and black, and yellow are soft and of just the right hue. The tableau reveals an excellence unequalled in our world, perhaps due to our turning away from the impulses of our blood to seek the novel, the unnatural.

Heed the call.

New emotions swell in Clark's breast, almost lifting his feet off of the ground. The pulse of thousands of generations throbs in him, making him dizzy. A deeper abyss than that at Stonehenge yawns before him. This is more primordial. His mind seeks to recoil from such vastnesses of time and kinship, but he stills himself. From some untapped reservoir proceeds the thought: I am of these. These are my people.

He would thus remain for much longer if Alistair did not call him back to our world: "They are only one of several threads."

He lets the statement linger there, without explanation. Clark is intrigued. "Threads?"

"The threads of the tapestry that comprises the European of today. From many times and many places they came to these lands, and with a myriad of inclinations, dispositions, gods, and customs. All spilled into that cauldron of transmutation that is Europa. For despite their sundry ways, the terrain and clime of these lands shaped them, forcing a broad uniformity upon them with the aid of time. The white winters, the gentle springtimes, the bright midsummers, the yellow autumns, the forests, the mountains, the secret groves, the mistletoe, the bears, the wolves, the roe buck: all conjoined to serve as agents for the creation of a people of a particular stamp."

As Alistair speaks, Clark's inner eye beholds scenes summoned both by the words and the glow of the cave with its frescoes. He sees tribes of human beings clad in animal skins arriving from all directions. Some cross the thin partition between Asia Minor and Europe when it was a mere trickle of water. Some sail the great middle sea northward from Africa into the underside of the continent. Others, on horseback and with an unyielding will marked on their brow, ride westward across the grasslands north of the Black Sea and the Caspian Sea. Clark discerns by a means unknown to him that these movements of people introduced a motley of beliefs and customs adding variety, like seasonings added to a stew heating on the mantle.

Clark also sees them change physical appearances. Blue eyes, green eyes, and hazel eyes flourish where previously brown had predominated. Hair color undergoes a similar slow transformation from dark brown to blonde and red and other lighter shades. Those who journeyed far into the north underwent the most drastic changes in their aspect. Bodies once dowdy and stout acquired angularity. Skin became fairer as well. Many grew taller. These permutations were not strictly localized, and variations appeared throughout the continent, but some areas favored specific traits. "My goodness, they're morphing right in front of me!" Clark thinks excitedly.

Alistair holds something in his hand and offers it to Clark. It is a spear fashioned in an ancient manner. The spear tip is of flint inserted into a slot and tied by rough cord to the shaft. The length almost matches Clark's height. Clark looks at it first, then at Alistair questioningly.

"Now is your chance to be brave, to be a man, as you wished. Take it, boy."

Without pausing to ask for meanings, Clark takes the weapon and wraps the fingers of both hands tightly around it. The coolness and smoothness of the wood thrill. Alistair then gently places his hands on his shoulders and turns him to face a dark part of the cave. Through some strange process, one of the bison has appeared there. Yet, it is not an ordinary bison. It shimmers like a mirage in the hot sun, its form semi-corporeal, allowing the eye to see through it, like a ghost.

Clark understands. He walks two paces away from Alistair,

choosing his own ground. He places his left hand forward and right hand back on the spear. His feet are slightly more than shoulder width apart, and he lowers his level slightly, like a wrestler's stance. He looks directly at the beast, into its eyes. This is my moment, he thinks. Nothing before this has had any meaning, and nothing after will if I do not acquit myself well here.

The animal paws the ground. Its docile nature has been aroused and substituted for a mounting aggression. It will charge the boy. The boy knows it. Clark's heart beats fast and his hands are cold, but he does not give ground. He feels his chest moving with each breath. A test he has longed for is finally being administered, and the bison is the proctor. He ought to be shaking, but he is not. Something beyond himself steadies him. Clark apprehends by a higher intuition that a cloud of witnesses now stands beside him. His ancestors and his ancestors' people are assembled for the trial. It is they who now brace him. Clark feels them like a cold breeze blowing through him, awakening his senses. Stern faces are looking at him from a distance. Hardened bodies standing in a mass face him. His thoughts have shriveled, leaving only the single necessity of the moment: stand your ground and fight.

Heed the call.

The bison paws the dirt three times in rapid succession then charges. Clark yells from a throat that has been waiting to cry out. He too charges. The spear is held unwaveringly in front of him, just below his eye level, not going left or right. He seeks the beast's heart. Amidst the snorting and the rising of the dust and the yelling, the two come together then —

Clark is suddenly alone at the dark end of the cavern. His breathing and his heartbeat rise and fall with force. His hands, which were solid in their purpose, now quake. The animal has disappeared. Just before contact, the bison evaporated into mist. Clark felt himself propelled through an empty space that contained a power that coursed through him and made him gasp.

Now he turns and sees Alistair where he left him. The older man does not grin or frown, but regards the boy with a serious look, like a father anxious to see his son prove himself in a contest he himself once persevered in. Alistair's gravity satisfies Clark. He feels honored in a way unlike any other in his boyhood. He feels proud of himself, as if he has earned a place among a higher rank. Chest still heaving, he holds the spear in his right hand and walks back to his original spot.

He stands in front of Alistair and waits for him to speak, spear planted in the dusty earth. Alistair claps a hand on Clark's shoulder and looks into his eyes, smiles, then says, "That was brilliant, Clark, brilliant. You have passed the first of several tests. I was not allowed to inform you of this test, and so I avoided your question when you asked a few days ago. But no matter. You have just proved yourself worthy, that is all that counts. I'm proud of you boy." He claps him several more times on the shoulder for emphasis.

Clark feels a tightness in his throat. He wants to hug Alistair but senses this would be inappropriate and restrains himself. "What does it all mean?" he asks.

"It means that you have begun the trials that transform a boy into a man. That is really what you want, isn't it? The satisfaction of knowing you are a man, and being respected by other men?"

"Yeah, I mean 'yes.' It feels like in our modern world boys just keep being boys. Some of the adult men I meet seem kind of childish, like they never really grew up. I don't want to be like them. But I'm not sure how to get to be the kind of man I have in mind. And then this happened. It feels, I don't know, right. I feel good, like this is what a man ought to be doing."

"You are correct in so many ways. Your world has turned its back on healthy, meaningful traditions, traditions that used to shape men and women. Take a young girl and make her a proper woman, or a young boy and man him up. A lot of the restlessness you feel is because your body and mind still crave the hardships that turn boys into men. This is one of the unfortunate byproducts of the technological age, although technology itself is neither good nor evil. A population that has severed themselves from the clear, crystal waters of subterranean streams that once refreshed them seeks refreshment elsewhere, in unwholesome, rotten places. They seek to satisfy the ancient cravings in sordid ways, never quite understanding why their shiny objects do not fulfill them."

"But why am I *different*?"

"The answer to that will be revealed in time, perhaps, but not by me, but by she who does the selecting."

"'She?'"

Alistair only grins, which indicates to Clark that the time for asking questions is at an end. The older man seems to enjoy the curiosity he has aroused and revels in it for a time, and Clark can't help but smile himself at the sport his mentor makes of the issue.

"Are you hungry, my young warrior?"

"Starving!"

"Let's go prepare a proper luncheon."

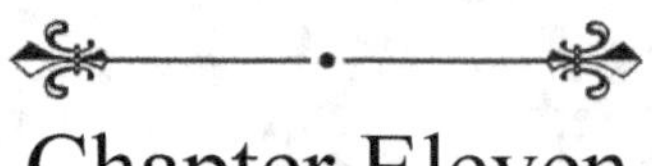

Chapter Eleven

That night as Clark lays contemplating the stars, he beholds another prodigy. The constellations shine brightly and he exults at finding different patterns when he notices movement among them. Some of the stars begin to rearrange themselves into new patterns. Slowly, Clark realizes that he is looking at a starry map of Europe. The brightest stars form the borders of the continent. The size of the map is enormous, filling almost half the sky. The rest of the stars begin forming themselves on the right, to the east of Europe, where one would expect to find Asia. From this location, they take turns spilling inside of the starry map. Once inside, they group themselves into shimmering lines. The lines then shoot across the continent in different directions like fireworks. Some of the starry arrows fly into the heart of Germany and there take up a kind of pulsation. This process repeats throughout the landmass. Others shoot up into Scandinavia and commence a similar pulsing. Poland, Romania, Hungary and the rest of Eastern Europe receive their payload of celestial lights, as well as Greece, Macedonia, Serbia, Croatia, Slovenia, Austria, and Bosnia. Far away Portugal and Spain receive a concentration of luminous visitors as well as France, many of them clustering around the north of Spain and the Pyrenean border with France. Eventually some leap across the channel into Britain and Ireland and find their own nesting areas inside those isles.

The star clusters swirl in a kind of agitation within their respective new homes for a while, then suddenly some splinter off, and thus begins a second and a third round of shooting lines of stars from one shining cluster to another region of the map. This development continues until the map is filled with various nodes of lights that have found permanent homes and vibrate in place, mostly around rivers. The Rhine, the Danube, the Dniester, the Dnieper, the Loire, the Ebro, the Thames, and the Shannon effervesce with starriness. The shooting movements slow but do not altogether cease. The final result is a map that vibrates with sparkly life and occasional eruptions of light bursts from one region to another.

Among the silvery stars there are a few red. These attract Clark's attention with a peculiar fascination, and his eyes track their movement with a deeper interest. The scarlet stars join in the regular streaking motions at first, until eventually they find permanent or at least semi-permanent territories. Clark witnesses their migrations into northern Germany on the Baltic coast, into England's Midlands, into a few clusters in Sweden by the Dal River. There are fewer red lights scattered in various other spots in the Mediterranean countries, and fewer still among the foothills of the Carpathians and the Balkans.

With a second sight that has become familiar, Clark knows these red stars to be his ancestors. As the realization dawns, his eyes grow larger and he follows the trails of his kin as they flash across the night sky. He thinks, "I'm seeing a constellation made of my family!" A yearning grows in his chest to rise up into the heavens and sup with his people, but he knows it is a vain dream even as he ponders it. Still, he follows his heart and surrenders to the fancy. As he does so, as he stretches out his longing, he begins to hear them. It begins as the trickling of a stream in a shady wood, then gradually rises to the crashing of waves on a rocky promontory. They are the voices, the aspirations, the heart-cravings of thousands of men and women in Clark's bloodlines. They seem to know him, and he senses rather that sees them smiling down at him, happy to be so willingly remembered by one of their own who now walks the Earth.

That night Clark falls asleep under a blanket of familial warmth and love radiated out of a heavenly realm that is a mirror of our own. Tears of thankfulness fall down his face as he wordlessly mouths his gratitude: "Thank you, thank you, thank you…"

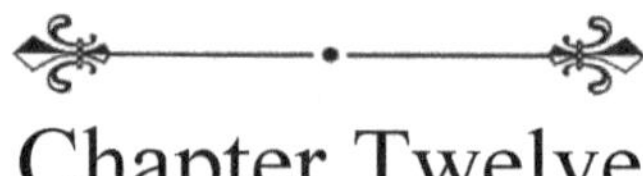

Chapter Twelve

Over the next few days Clark and Alistair wander the surrounding landscape of outside of this cave in northern Spain. Just as before, Clark notices the lack of buildings, automobiles, and people, but says nothing. He worries that asking might ruin the present tranquility, and so diligently maintains his accustomed quiet. I probably talk too much in general, he considers, and proposes to himself that he will thenceforward speak less and thus enjoy more.

The duo's regular itinerary features hiking, exploring caves, learning the names of trees and plants and rocks, fishing, fording streams, finding bird's nests, and many other activities pertaining to the outdoors. Clark grasps that Alistair is reinforcing the lessons learned first at Stonehenge and then at the Altamira cave. Namely, that it is meet that he, Clark, should enfold himself within the garments woven from the terrain and animalia of Europe which underlie the experience of his people. Every leaf of every tree, every petal of every flower, every birdsong, connects Clark to entire nations as they have traveled through time. Now I can talk to them about things that we both understand, Clark thinks. His education in the wild is a debt of honor he owes his kin who spent so much time in wood and dale.

And so days pass and Clark's senses sharpen just as his body hardens. He was never a flaccid boy, but now his muscles ache in a new and invigorating way. After the aches subside they leave stronger muscles. He can move heavier weight without becoming winded. He can climb steep embankments with greater stamina. He focuses on keeping his breathing at a normal rhythm in spite of physical labor. New vistas unfold before him of a larger awareness, of a dawning manhood. He seeks out hardships as trials of his robustness. Can I get to the top of this hill without panting? Can I handle this prickly bramble without wincing? Can I walk erect without slouching from fatigue? How do I compare to my ancestors? Would they be proud of me if they met me? These are the thoughts of a young boy raised in the softness of an industrialized world far away from the wet, morning chill of dark forests.

"How are you feeling lately Clark?" Alistair asks one day.

"Healthy and strong. Brave." Clark's speech begins to take on the aspect of his growth, substituting childish constructions like "I'm feeling great" for more mature speech.

"I note that also. You are becoming more and more every day a man of the woods." To be described as a man makes Clark's chest swell. "You realize there will be future trials, do you not?"

"Yes."

"Do you feel prepared?"

"I do."

"Why?"

"Because of what the stones told me and what the cave taught me. I know I don't know everything yet, but I have a base, a foundation to work on now. A foundation I didn't have before. I feel confident, and if I ever don't feel confident, I know where to go to feel strong."

Alistair weighs these words with what appears to Clark like approval. He puffs sweet-smelling clouds of smoke from his pipe as the two lounge at the base of a young beech tree glowing with sunrays upon its light green leaves. The two have finished a meal of trout and now sit amidst the leavings. Alistair leans against the trunk of the beech and Clark props himself up on his arms, occasionally shifting position. He wears a billowy white shirt with the sleeves rolled up to his elbows. The older man tends his pipe, which occasionally requires re-lighting. His light grey tweed shows little sign of wear and remains mostly unwrinkled. At times he removes the red pocket square and reshapes it. His legs are stretched out and his brown boots shine from the buffing Alistair conferred upon them earlier. When he pulls his arms behind his head to enjoy a good stretch his red and white suspenders are seen hugging his torso.

"We are soon going to meet people. Those we meet are individuals who have contributed greatly to our civilization. I will leave you temporarily in their care and return for you later. Do not be dismayed by my leave-takings, you will be well attended."

"I'm not worried about it." This was mostly true, for although Clark has come to see Alistair as a bulwark against the unknown, he wants to be brave on his own.

"That's good, that's good. I know you're not worried. Courage has grown in you. Yet I wish to impress upon you the following: Strive always to show yourself a respectful, courteous page."

Clark's brows furrow. "A page?"

"A young man in training to become a knight is called a page. Afterwards, when he reaches a certain stage he becomes a squire, then finally a knight."

Clark's eyes widen. "You mean…?"

Alistair laughs. "No, not quite. I'm not suggesting we are making you into a knight as such, but your path resembles that of a knight in some respects, so I used knighthood as a comparison. And as a page, it is expected that you conduct yourself according to the principles of chivalry. Now, you are already a well-natured young lad, respectful and kind, but I would be remiss if I did not seek to reinforce the importance of a chivalrous spirit."

"I want everyone who meets me to think of me like that. I *want* to be chivalrous. I want to be respected." This last sentiment embarrasses Clark right after the words leave his mouth, although he is not sure why.

"Ha ha! That's perfectly normal, for a man to crave *respect*. It's healthy and *natural*, that. Just as long as it does not become pride. Now there's the challenge facing all of us men. Pride is a temptation you will wrestle with your whole *life*."

With each conversation Clark feels his understanding widening like ripples on a quiet pond agitated by a small pebble. In his case, a pond of ignorance and innocence struck by a pebble of wisdom. He not only grasps the meaning of Alistair's words but also interprets the manner in which they are spoken. Every emphasis, every pause, everything left unsaid is weighed on the scales of Clark's growing comprehension. Thus the boy creeps towards manhood like a sapling taking in nutrients from the soil and sunlight and rainwater.

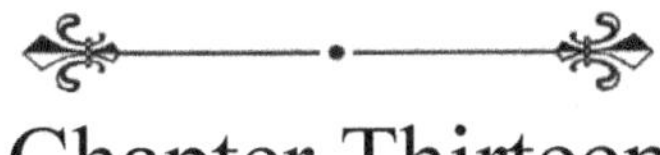

Chapter Thirteen

Dear reader, before continuing our story, I wish to take you up and out of the adventures of Clark and Alistair and view their story from above, as it were. For just as you have been following their course, others have as well. A kind of invisible college attends to their goings-on, as well as that of others making similar journeys. One member of this hidden society you have already met. Her name is Sophia, and she guides our young page and his tutor by means of inspirations, intuitions, as well as direct communication. She is even now assessing Clark's progress. She takes into consideration his eagerness, his passion, his commitment to his own inborn sense of chivalry, and his overall temperament. She guides, but does not coerce. Clark might meet her at some point, but this remains to be decided, as it is much too soon in his tutelage to determine this yet. Also, meeting Sophia in a direct face-to-face encounter is reserved for a small elect of those who currently walk the earth. Alistair, as you might have guessed, is out of our world yet in it. Thus he regularly confers with members of the hidden society. Clark must walk a long road before he can even be considered. But we shall see.

For now, let us hover a little behind Sophia's shoulder and see what she sees and hear what she hears. This is perfectly acceptable: she wants us with her.

*   *   *

"Hi! I'm glad you could join me." She smiles at us with soft pink lips and small dimples. "I want you to know that everything I wish for Clark — happiness, goodness, a sense of purpose, fidelity to a code of honor — all this and more I want also for you. There is a light inside of you. My sister Lucy lit it on orders from on high. It wants to burn brightly. Don't you want it to burn?" Her smile grows as she tells us of her affection for us.

She speaks to us as she looks down through what appears to be a large crystal window, as long as a tree is tall and as wide as three men standing on top of one another. Through the glass we see the Earth, and we see the many boys and girls who are on paths like Clark, each with guides like Alistair. Some of them are from Europe, others, like Clark, are from the former colonies: Australia, Canada, New Zealand, South Africa, and the US. They are in different stages of their training. Some are struggling, others thriving. We see them suddenly grow large before us, like ghostly transparent figures, then shrink down again to make room for others. Thus we come to witness the pupils that comprise the school of the hidden society.

"I wasn't always a watcher. I was down there on Earth like you. I was a girl in a happy home with a loving father and mother. I was blessed. Our home was large and comfortable, with tall cypresses lining it on both sides. It was a bright, white house on a hill at the end of a winding road that sometimes got dusty in the summer. Visitors would arrive and our servants would clean off the road dirt while someone would get father and others would prepare a table. Father was usually reading in our library or talking and sharing his thoughts with mother. He would greet our guests with a hearty 'Hello' and make them feel at home right away. When everyone was seated and the wine and fruit and cheeses were served on silver trays, I would be called for. I was the only child for a long time. I was happy to meet new people and make sure *they* were happy in our home. Father would say, 'And this is my pride and joy, the light of our home, my girl Sophia.' I would always *blush*! Mother would smile and softly chide father, 'Polyxeinus, don't embarrass her,' but I wasn't really that embarrassed. I knew they loved me.

"Then we would talk and ask questions about what was happening in our part of Greece. I lived in a region called Elis. That's where I was born, on the shores of the Ionian Sea. It was before the great events that would shake our little island people: the wars with the Persians, the horrible wars between Spartans and Athenians. We lived right around the time little Greece was crawling out of its dark ages. It was mostly peaceful in our corner. And everyone respected my father, which added to our harmony. He was an honest man, a good man, always helping others. He was descended from heroes who had fought at Troy with Achilles and Odysseus.

"One day it happened that I fell sick. I was in bed and thought it was just a springtime fever that would pass in time. But as I lay there

I began to sense that I wasn't alone. I began to hear whispers, to feel presences. I wasn't frightened, but curious. I felt that something important was going to happen. I found out later that my parents were having dreams at the same time. They were being visited by forces who told them to be strong, because soon their daughter would be taken from them. But they must not fret, the voices said, because I had been selected for a special purpose. Although I would be gone, I would still be with my parents, but in a different form. None of this was very clear to me at the time, although I had a faint sense that I knew what was meant, as if I had been waiting for this my whole life."

As Sophia speaks, we see the students going about their trials and living their experiences through the glass portal. Most of them are young, about Clark's age. A few are in their late teens, and a much smaller proportion are in their twenties. The tutors assigned to each student are men and women of multifarious backgrounds. Some are middle-aged, bearded men of serious, academic mien, some are young men of strong frame and athletic proportions with confidence on their faces, some are women of aristocratic stamp in elegant dress with hair neatly arranged as if by ladies-in-waiting, some are grandmotherly matrons with beautifully lined faces.

Sophia regards them all with a benign expression that never wavers. She wears a perpetual smile that grows or diminishes, but never completely fades. Now it is at its resting position, a faint upturning of the corners of her mouth. Her eyes also smile. She is like a young girl eagerly awaiting the arrival of a new sibling so she can pour out her love over him: a river of affection and warmth that ever spills its abundance on the disheartened.

"On my final night on Earth, my parents were at my bedside. The candles threw shadows on the walls and on the curtains that gently swayed and seemed to share in the sadness of the moment. I had already said goodbye to our servants whom I loved like family members. The house was very still. Far away I heard night owls and dogs barking in the hills. I wondered if I would enjoy the little details of life such as these in my new life.

"As I lay looking into the eyes of my mother and father, there came a moment when we knew it was time. I said 'I love you' with my eyes, then they closed, never again to open in that body." Here Sophia pauses momentarily, and a brief sadness touches her lips and eyes as she recalls her farewell.

After a reflective moment, she resumes, "What came next is difficult to describe in human terms, except to say there was a loss of heaviness and a release. Then I met beautiful beings and spoke with them, not with words, but with the mind, in a new way. I learned the reasons for my being chosen and what my duties were to be.

"I watch over the children of Europa as a gardener tends a garden. All the plants and trees and flowers that I oversee grow out of the rich soil that is Europa. This soil bears the nutrients of successive waves of men and women who have come here and undergone the weathering effects of these lands. As the land assimilated them, they shed their former attributes or saw these transformed. Through a slow, organic process, these new characteristics entered into the soil of the European spirit to become the common property of all. Thus resulted a people of various outward appearances and dispositions who nevertheless share a collective nourishment.

"Out of this garden bloom flowers of uncommon beauty and grace. One never knows when they will bloom, so I keep a close watch. These blossoms draw into themselves all that is best of the shared patrimony of Europe. All the excellences of intelligence, imagination, heroism, beauteous form, clarity — all conjoin into the stem, the petals, the pistils, the stamens. Each flower is a velvety radiance of whites and pinks and lavenders, of azures and crimsons. No flower is only of one color, most are of two. Some reveal even more variety.

"When I see one, I send out workers to cultivate these blossoms. They tend to them, make sure no harm comes to them from violent weather or pests. My latest discovery is a gorgeous blossom named Clark." She turns and winks at us as she says his name.

*   *   *

Dear reader, we shall leave our gracious gardener to her work for now. But do not despair — know that she watches over us still.

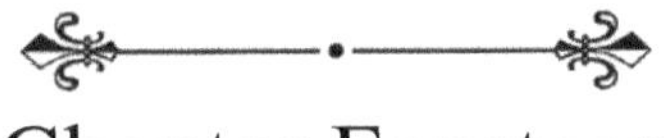

Chapter Fourteen

It is a day of departure again for Clark and Alistair. The boy has catalogued several genus of flora and fauna and wildlife by sight, and he begins to feel that the woods are a second home. Alistair has leant him a knife, which he uses to clean the fish he catches. "Can we hunt land animals and can I learn how to gut them too?" he asks eagerly. Alistair just laughs and says, "Perhaps in time, my aspiring woodsman. But not this round. We have more travels ahead. People to meet. Places to explore."

Clark reads his book throughout this interim. He takes it with him into the woods, finds a snug depression in the forest floor, nestles himself into it, and enjoys a few pages. Sometimes he backs against a tree. He has finished the first three chapters. These deal with the waves of migration funneled over ages into that pointy promontory sticking out into the Atlantic, the terminus of a prodigious landmass. Like a dynamo of transformation, the tireless little smithy that is Europe sparked and crackled out a relentless toil over its anvil that spanned millennia. The chapters touch briefly upon the Neanderthal epoch and the contributions left by our distant cousins during their Middle Paleolithic sojourn. Clark's imagination, ignited by images of tools made using the Levallois technique and of tidy burial sites, travels back to these furthest ancestors to have flattened European grasslands. Did they think and feel like us? Were they anxious or placid? What was the meaning of an elderberry bush through their eyes?

Other sections dealt with the arrival of homo sapiens and the long trajectory of their ascent. A flourishing of artwork and technology erupts with these gifted new arrivals. The two groups overlap for several millennia, and undoubtedly interact with each other. Again Clark can't help but conjecture about this commingling of human tribes. What did they think about one another? How did they differ in the way they saw nature? Was one more spiritual than the other? Was one happier? Did a starry sky mean the same to both?

As much as we would like to leave Clark happily musing, events force us on. The day came when Alistair said to him, "Get your things together and prepare, we must sail on." Clark accepted this easily, almost eagerly, because of an awareness of ripeness. Yes, it is time to move on. He has softly trod the sandy shores of his new world and must now cast off. He washes his clothes in a cold clear stream and bathes his body there as well. He hangs his garments on a line stretched between two beeches and the sun dries them. The pair break camp without speaking, silently tidying and storing. When all is packed and neat, Alistair invites Clark to sit by him on a rock shaped like a bench just out of the shade of a nearby tree.

"Our next phase is going to involve more one-on-one interaction between you and some special individuals, like I explained. First we are going to stand on a kind of observation post, so to speak, and get the lay of the land. Then we will proceed directly into the thick of things. We will be firmly within the realm of the Indo-European and his worldview."

Clark's eyebrows raise a little and he asks with interest, "Who exactly are the Indo-Europeans?"

"They are the most direct members of our family, Clark. We are their grandchildren you might say, whereas all the other tribes are distant relatives removed from us by vaster chasms. You will see much more that reminds you of you among these Indo-Europeans, but your ears will still hear the distant echo of the cave painters and the stone sculptors." Alistair smiles then abruptly gets up. "Let's have tea then and say our farewells to this Iberian idyll."

Alistair puts the kettle on the boil and the two delight in their cups. Then Alistair says to Clark, "Let's have a look at the book then."

Clark removes his book from his satchel. "Now turn to chapter four." Clark does so. The chapter opens with a glossy full-page illustration of a god with wild, flowing white hair and imposing bare chest wielding jagged thunderbolts in his hand and glaring at something below him as he hurtles forward in a golden chariot pulled by demented horses through a darkling cloudy sky. "Place your hand on the page." Clark does so unhesitatingly and Alistair follows suit. The boy glances up at his mentor without showing fear and Alistair looks at the boy. Then all is in motion.

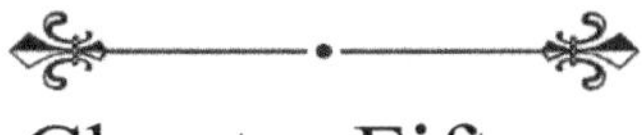

Chapter Fifteen

small wooden bridge of cherry wood spans a gently flowing brook. The brook is bordered by reeds that are not quite as tall as a man. The cool water flows over smooth rounded rocks not larger than the palm of your hand. Its movement is slow enough to allow a clear observation of the stones. The beams of the bridge are thick and sturdy, scrupulously fashioned with care. Clark and Alistair stand on the bridge facing the sun looking at a tapestry of black woven material. The garment lazily flutters in the light breeze at an angle away from the viewers. The tapestry shows a map of Europe stitched with dark golden thread. There are no country borders, just as there were none in the stellar map. To the east of Europe teems a mass of yellow lights that look like a paste made of yellow suns compressed together. The mass seems like a living, throbbing thing. It appears to be facing the west, peering into the interior of Europe with craving, heaving with the expectation of pushing westward. The yellow glow pulsates like the breast of a buck deer who has just bounded away from a crunching sound in the woods.

"You are looking at one of the most significant migrations in world history. Those," Alistair points with his pipe, "are the Indo-Europeans."

The cloud of gilded shimmering continues breathing heavily until suddenly there is a pause of about three heartbeats. Then a rushing ensues, as comet-shaped effusions of the glowing haze thrust themselves into northern India and neighboring Persia, which appear barely in the lower right-hand corner of the tapestry-map, and into nearly every recess of Europe. Clark sees into the thick soup of condensed suns and beholds the peopling of the occident. He sees fierce war chiefs with tattoos and sinewy limbs, sternly talking with forest-dwellers of the dark Bavarian woods, with hard-scrabble farmers among the coarse brush of the Peloponnese, and with a vigorous tribe of brightly clad men and women close to the Baltic shore in Latvia. The scene is repeated throughout the mainland and on some islands as well. The recently arrived Indo-Europeans displace the local populations either with violence or threat of violence. Sometimes they scatter the people just by the rumor of their appearance. In place of established traditions, new traditions appear, sometimes effacing, sometimes amalgamating. Old gods and goddesses are relegated to secondary positions when they are not altogether forgotten. Old ways of growing and gathering food make way for a more aggressive ethos of hunting and animal breeding. A largely pacific way of life finds itself upended by a warrior aristocracy. The Indo-Europeans have arrived, and they bristle with the pride of life. All is hot lust and vigor.

Clark has been leaning forward ever slowly, drawn in with the beholding of this ransacking. He nearly topples but catches himself, and clears his throat. "Alistair, I feel more connected to these people than to any others. These really are OUR people, aren't they?"

"Yes, Clark, they are our most immediate ancestors, although those who came before them have a claim on us as well, just not as direct. The very language we are speaking, English, can be traced back to them by means of a twisting, winding path. Almost every European god and mythology you ever heard of was brought to Europe by them. The old gods, the ones belonging to the subjugated people, did not die out in every case: sometimes they became the devils of the underworld, or an ancient race of enemy deities defeated by the newcomers. Old monuments, such as dolmens and cairns, took on new meanings when occupied by the vigorous newcomers. Just as the forest floor is constantly nourished by falling leaves and pinecones, so too the fleshly sediment of Europe—its people—has constantly been fed by sturdy races. And just like the trees and plants of soggy forests, the newcomers have undergone a process of decomposition and growth, releasing and taking in nutrients, growing into new life."

Clark feels more strongly than during his previous encounters a stirring of blood and memory. It is like seeing a photo album of relatives removed by only two or three generations in comparison to portraits of distant ancestors hung in a gallery. The force of recognition is unmistakable now. He longs to see them up close and observe their activity.

"Are you ready to meet some people now Clark?"

"Yes! Yes! That's all I can think about."

"Right then. We are going to them then. I will introduce you to some of them, and as I said before, leave you in their care. They are ambassadors of their cultures, who have been chosen as worthy representatives of their people. They are aware of you, and of other students like you. They've taken others under their wings before, although they have not ventured upon same course of education you are about to venture upon.

"Be brave and be courteous. Remember to listen more than you speak, for this is good manners.

"You won't be traveling via the usual manner," Alistair indicates the book. "I'll keep it safe so it won't weigh you down. You'll need your dexterity where you're going.

"Now I want you to focus your eyes there," and Alistair points at a place on the billowing map where a white light begins glowing out from the surrounding goldenness. The light radiates from a spot near the center of the map. Clark later learns it is the Black Forest in Germany.

"Send your intention to that spot and do not release it until you have arrived at your destination. I will join you in good time. Be brave, be strong. Now, focus!"

Clark does as he is told. He looks intently at the light. Soon it begins growing, then it is all around him, and he barely sees anything else. The light then begins to diminish, revealing a new land. He is no longer standing on the bridge next to Alistair. He now stands under an enormous, sturdy beech tree with a thick covering of leaves in a dim forest. Insects drone lazily all around him. His eyes seek to penetrate the gloom of this darkest of forests Clark has yet experienced, but there is nothing to see beyond more trees and muted sunlight. There is a feeling of power here, as of a kingdom of noble trees who have grown slightly insolent through ages of dominion. Indeed, the oldest denizens of this leafy realm saw the coming and going of the last ice sheets, so hoary is their lineage.

Standing there, Clark breathes deeply. He seeks to steady himself against the feeling of denseness given off by the woodland. He wishes there were someone next to him so he would not feel like a lone human intruder. Just then he hears a voice behind him, to his right. "You have finally arrived, young one."

Book Two

In the field of battle, it is disgraceful for the chief to be surpassed in valor; it is disgraceful for the companions not to equal their chief; but it is reproach and infamy during a whole succeeding life to retreat from the field surviving him. To aid, to protect him; to place their own gallant actions to the account of his glory, is their first and most sacred engagement. The chiefs fight for victory; the companions for their chief.

— Tacitus, <u>Germania</u>

Chapter One

Clark twirls around, only slightly startled, as he had anticipated a meeting. Before him stands one who emanates manful vitality. He is bare chested and wears a brown leather belt fastened with a knot. His breeches are of tan wool, his footwear two slips of leather tied around the toes and ankles. His torso is wiry and muscular, and there are three scars running across his left breast and midsection. His hair is long and darkish blonde and is tied with a band made from river reeds. His eyes are of the bluest hue Clark has ever seen in a person, and they stare out of a visage that does not know nonsense. From his hairline down to his chin his features are a flow of regularity. Generations of hardihood served to produce this specimen of flawlessness. His brow with its two bulging veins sits like a fortress above his eyes, his jawline inclines downward tautly to his chin, and his thin lips stretch with seriousness. He regards the boy steadily.

Clark begins to speak, but has to clear his voice. "Hello. My name is Clark."

"Yes, I know. Alistair has told me. Are you ready to begin?"

Clark does not know what the man means, but he feels that asking questions at this moment would be foolish and make him appear weak, so he answers yes.

"Follow me," the man says, and turns around and walks towards the west. Clark follows.

As Clark walks behind, he observes all with a heightened alertness, like before in the cave. He sends out his vision like a scout to inspect every crease in the bark of trees, every undulation in the ground, every animal movement in the branches, all the twigs and pinecones on the forest floor. He applies what he has learned. He scans the ground where his foot will fall as well as what is in front of him. He tries to anticipate the rise and fall of the land. He listens for signs of animals and periodically looks behind him to make sure he is not being tracked. He smells the scents of the woodland and attempts to distinguish among them: pine, wild lilac, wet earth. The crunch of leaves under his feet soothes.

He strives to keep pace with his new guide without showing signs of fatigue, even as beads of sweat break out on his forehead. He moderates his breathing, lengthens his strides, assumes control of his body. He does not speak during their trek through the woods.

After nearly an hour of walking, they come over a swelling in the ground and behold a village by a gently flowing stream. The houses are circular with thatched roofs. Smoke billows from the center of some dwellings. Men and women mill about, busy with various tasks. Some tend to animal hides stretched over wooden frames. Others repair clothing. Small groups of men converse and gesture with their hands, excitedly recounting the recent boar hunt. Groups of boys handle spears in mock combat until yelled at by a stern gray bearded man.

Clark and his guide walk right to the largest construction, a kind of hall with thick lumber projecting out from the roof. Clark is told to wait outside. The man reappears soon afterwards with three other men. Two of them seem the same age as the first, about twenty-five or thirty summers, but the third man seems old enough to be their father. All of them are dressed similarly, with brown, earthen tones. The older man wears a necklace of animal teeth. His right shoulder bears a tattoo of black wavy patterns. The trio regard their visitor intently, assessing him. Clark tries to hold their gazes with neither nervousness nor insolence.

The older man speaks: "What do you wish to learn here, boy?"

Without pausing, Clark answers, "My heritage and my place in the world of men, sir."

The old man continues looking directly into Clark's eyes. Clark tries not to blink. "Supply him with his necessities, Gunthari, and prepare him for the trials."

Clark's guide, whose name he has finally learned, grunts assent. He tells Clark to follow him and the two leave for Gunthari's dwelling. The old man and the two younger ones exchange glances but say nothing.

*   *   *

"What do you think of your young charge, Alistair, as he approaches his new trials?" Sophia asks the older Scotsman the question with her usual cheerful grin. This always enlivens the old Scot, and he responds with good cheer.

"Oh, I'm both fond of and confident in our boy, Sophie." Their friendship over the centuries has fostered this familiarity. "His heart is pure, or at least, as pure as a young boy in his distressed age can be. And good blood flows in him, filling his heart with noble purpose. He craves what we are offering him, and I do not think he will easily abandon his path, in spite of difficulty. At any rate, enduring hardship is fundamental."

"Indeed it is, beloved brother. Such is the decree of Heaven, and we children of Heaven must adhere to its dictates. Although it need not be an ordeal. Not always. The heart can be softened and made receptive to the One Path. That is why I am glad you are in charge of our Clark, knowing what you endured and how you endured. I'm very happy about this pairing, aren't you?"

How could Alistair do other than agree with the dark-haired beauty and her words of encouragement? "Yes Sophie, I am indeed happy with my assignment, and I thank you as always for your judgment and trust in me."

Grinning with her whole visage, Sophia bestows her blessing upon Alistair and speeds him on his way.

Chapter Two

Clark wakes up not knowing where he is. He hears birdsong before his eyes open. Their notes are new and pleasant, and because unfamiliar, provoke curiosity. Then his lids open and he beholds rustic wood furniture hewn with economy of labor yet soothing in its simplicity. He also looks out of a small window at green leaves on a branch that bobs with the wind. Slowly, he remembers. Today is his first day of the "trials," whatever they may be. He must steel himself, he thinks, but not become insensitive to the wonder of it all. "If I get too tough, I might not see the beauty of this world, and that would be a shame," the boy ponders in his heart. He must find a balance, he decides, between hard necessity and poetic abandon. He wants Alistair to be proud of him and not disappointed, and this strengthens his resolve to harden himself. He also recalls the visions at Stonehenge and the cave, the voices, the *presence* of the unseen hosts, and these memories puff his heart with sustaining poesy. With these impressions revolving in his soul, he stirs himself from the floor where he has slept upon an animal hide.

Clark finds a homely table with a pitcher of water resting on it. It was not there the night before, so he infers it was left for his use. He drinks deeply, suddenly finding himself very thirsty. After quenching his thirst, he takes a look around his host's habitation. Gunthari's house is sparse: a bed of stacked hides and cushions filled with feathers, a low-lying bench, pegs on a wall from which hang weapons and shields. Two small windows on either side of the rectangular abode provide light, and an aperture above his head allows smoke to dissipate. There is little color apart from the woody hues of trees used in the manufacture of furniture and house. Clark expects to see something, but is not sure what. He continues to scan the room until he decides it is better to get started on the day's tasks.

Outside the hut he finds Gunthari sitting against a wall of the dwelling and working with something made of leather. With one hand he grips the end of a dark leather strap, with the other he shuttles a metal implement back and forth. Clark watches him with interest until he realizes the man is sharpening a blade. Gunthari does not look up from his chore when he addresses the boy.

"You slept well?"

"Yes."

"Even on the floor of a crude house?"

"I don't care. I want to be here."

Gunthari gives a small but seemingly satisfied laugh. "Then let's have our breakfast and we can talk about today's work."

After a few more strokes on the leather strop, Gunthari places his implements back inside his hut, hangs them on the wall with pegs, and walks out again where Clark is waiting.

The two amble to the village center. Billowing blue smoke emanates from a fire in the middle of the plaza. Several sturdy poles in the shape of connected triangles support slabs of roasting meat. Two men attend the cooking of the meal. Other village dwellers are standing or sitting around, talking in quiet tones. They are a reserved people, not inclined to flamboyance or loudness. Clark observes them as he approaches. The women are noticeably attractive, with fine, regular features in their faces and hair. Some have raven, dark locks, but Clark notices a tendency for fairness. Some bind their hair with small clips adorned with some silvery material, but other clips are adorned with red or black. Many braid their hair in tight twists and then fasten them in the back. Their bodies are angular and many are tall or of medium height. They wear flowing garments of light dun tied about the neck and upper chest with tawny strings, much like the bodices of a later period. Their manner of walking and talking is pleasant, neither timid or impudent, but self-assured, at peace with life, joyful and free. They smile at Clark as he comes into view, and every smile feels like an undeserved indulgence.

The daughters are comely as well, and Clark can't help but feel flustered as he feels their gaze upon him. He tries not to stare, but it is a struggle, as the girls his age are very pretty and invite admiration. Some of them huddle and talk in whispers full of mirth and suppressed laughter as Clark walks by, and this makes him redden. He notices one in particular, a brunette girl with a healthy ruddiness on her snowy cheeks, and as he walks by his eyes meet hers. Within an instant that lasts ages, he feels transported by a yearning such as he has never felt. Their eyes hold one another and communicate something of desire and something of completion. Clark's throat and chest constrict in an agony he would not want abated. For several paces he looks into those dark eyes under equally dark brows, not breathing, as she returns his gaze, following him as he transits across the plaza. A thought emerges in his mind, unbidden but immediately welcomed, from an unknown region in his heart: "Everything I do from this moment on I do for her. I must earn her."

Clark remains in a haze even as Gunthari motions him to be seated on a communal bench occupied by some men. The men might otherwise have unnerved him, had he not been beyond the reach of unnerving, with their fierce appearances. Most had tattooed bodies, some even tattooed faces. Their expressions were grim and serious more often than not, with lines running down their foreheads. Their hair was also usually long and either bound in the back near the crown of the head or, less commonly, braided. Not one was obese, but most were wiry and muscular. A few larger men carried their muscle like small cushions under their hides, and one might mistake them as overweight from a distance, but this illusion was quickly dispelled up close. Arguments were rare, as all knew their place in the social order and instinctually acquiesced to it. The men's faces tended towards elongation rather than roundness, with weather-bronzed cheeks and brows below which stared blazing blue or hazel or brown irises. Half the male population of the village wore grizzled, rough countenances, while the other half were graced with fine, smooth features. Gunthari belonged to this latter category. When they spoke, it was always with directness and frankness that would have seemed like insolence to outsiders. They measured their words so as to speak with economy, and not blather, which was considered womanish. They observed and listened more often than they spoke, and weighed all in order to convey succinctness and precision when it came time for speech. When they disciplined their children, they did not need to repeat themselves. The boys of the village tried to pattern themselves after such stern manly models, and conscientiously ridiculed their peers whose behavior deviated from the healthful norm.

Clark was dimly aware of the looks he received from the men at his table, and regulated his behavior in order to conform to the status quo as he understood it. Whatever timidity might have afflicted him was allayed by his experiences of the past weeks in Alistair's company as well as his recently kindled ardor for the dark-haired beauty. "I must be mindful of my behavior from now on, for she might be watching me." This was his thought as he settled himself down among the men at his table.

"Good day Gunthari," several of the men greeted Clark's guide. "Good day to you brothers."

"How does it go with the young one?"

Gunthari looks at Clark briefly with an appraising eye then answers, "It remains to be seen, but our young guest seems eager. We shall see."

Clark is even more resolved now to prove himself so that in future Gunthari need not hesitate when speaking of him. Come what may, he is ready, for his own honor, for his people, for Alistair, and for *her*. He sets his jaw and fixes his determination.

Soon the women and young maidens are bringing plates of steaming meat to the table of men. It is roasted boar, and its sweet scent makes Clark's mouth water. The cutlets drip with fat which pool on the platters. There are also loaves of a rather flattened bread, although not fully flat. These are distributed to each member of the table. Clark tries surreptitiously scanning the girls bringing the victuals to see if *she* is among them, but she does not appear.

Clark waits for the men to begin before touching his plate, for this seems fitting. When Gunthari picks up a portion of steaming meat Clark follows suit. The boar is seasoned with salt and some other flavorings he can't identify, although he has tasted it before. His mouth waters and momentarily he feels dizzy. "I am tasting food in its purest state prepared in the old, traditional style," he thinks, and the awareness almost makes him swoon. He feels engaged in this world more intimately than either at Stonehenge or in the Spanish cave by the sharing of a common meal cooked by the dwellers of a foregone age. He relishes the meal as he has never relished a meal before. The boar meat is juicy with fat and very tender, making chewing mostly unnecessary. It dissolves in his mouth and goes down easily. The bread complements the viand perfectly, with its slightly salty flavor and firm texture, preparing the palate for the next mouthful of sweet meat.

Clark temporarily forgets all else as he eats, lost in a culinary haze of obliviousness. He soon recovers himself and checks his posture at table and his overall manners. "Do you like it?" Gunthari asks.

"I love it."

Gunthari laughs and his teeth shimmer white against his sun-bronzed complexion. "Eat hearty, you will need your strength later."

"Yes sir."

"You can call me Gunthari. It was my father's name, and it is now mine, as I was the eldest born."

"Where are your siblings?"

"Some are dead, gone to be with our ancestors. One brother lives here, and two sisters are married to men of other villages."

Clark weighs this as he continues enjoying his meal. Pitchers of water are being distributed at the moment, and Clark is startled when the arm that sets the pitcher next to him belongs to his pretty girl. He looks up into her face and freezes as she looks down and into his eyes. She smiles and gives a soft laugh in reaction to his astonished expression. Clark perceives the heat radiating from his cheeks. As the girl retreats from the table, Clark reproves himself for his awkwardness and vows to be more self-possessed.

"Today you will be tested. All our boys are tested. It is necessary in order to make sure they become men. A boy who does not grow up to be a man is no good to anyone. Are you nervous?"

"A little, but I will control it."

"That is good. It is good to control fear, because you will always feel fear, even as a man. Some men do not, but they are born that way. Most of us do. It is normal, but it is also necessary to know how to defeat fear. This is the role of a man.

"The world you come from has forgotten how to make men. The men there are soft, like girls. I am ashamed when I think that this is the future of our bloodlines, but that is beyond my control. I am here to help you become the man you want to be, for that is why you are here. Alistair and I talked. He showed me your soul. You want to be strong. You want to be a man, not like the soft, womanish men of your time. That is good. That is how it should be. But it will be hard. You are ready to face the hardness and the fear?"

"Yes Gunthari."

The hard man nods his head in approval. "Whatever happens, tell yourself, 'I have a man's soul in me.' This will help you get through life." He looks down at his plate and devours another portion of the succulent pork. When he finishes, he wipes his mouth with the back of his hand and stands up. "Let us go."

Clark is escorted by Gunthari to a field just outside the village where a group of boys his age are assembling. Loose dirt and sand line the floor of the small enclosure. Clark removes his shirt to match the other boys, who are bare-chested. The murmuring and excited chatter cease when the old man who greeted Clark yesterday appears. He takes his place in front of the boys and scans their miens until silence reigns. Insolence is not tolerated here. The old man commences, "Young ones, you are gathered together again to continue your training to be men. As always, you are expected to take this seriously, for our tribe is alone in this world, and we have only ourselves to protect us. Sweep your hearts clean of nonsense, and invoke the All-Father, that he may dwell inside of a clean heart." At this the old man closes his eyes and breathes deeply, his brow furrowed in concentration. The boys mimic him. Clark also closes his eyes, and although he calls upon no deity, he draws upon the spiritual vigor generated by the gathering. He is utterly in earnest as to his purpose, and he follows his guiding thoughts. In his mind's eye he sees the pillar of strength he has erected to fortify himself during his sojourn away from home. He sees his father and mother and wishes to honor them for the love and sacrifice they have shown him. He sees the megaliths at Stonehenge and recalls the words he heard there. *Heed the call.* He sees the shadowy myriads of his kin from the vision in the cave and welcomes the compulsion to excel thus prompted. And now, as the latest addition to his interior column of power, he sees *her*, the anonymous beauty of the village. She now supersedes all other concerns in his young man's heart. It is for her, principally, that he must predominate. At all times he is acutely aware that she might be watching and assessing him, and this perception stimulates a constant alertness in Clark. He is a taut wire, ever vigilant. He has replaced his normally inquisitive manner with a single-pointed determination to prove himself the best man.

The test that Clark will undergo today is the result of a refined process sifted across generations by distant ancestors. The men of Gunthari's people have arrived at a precise understanding of manhood and of humanity's place in the world, and have never seen the need to modify their conclusions. Their premises rest upon certain manifest observations. First, life is hard. That is manifest. Who can gainsay it? Next, men are called upon to engage the hardness of life. This too is manifest. What other option is available? Promoting or allowing weakness in a harsh world is unthinkable. And finally the third postulate which follows from the first two: boys must be schooled to become men capable of coping with the hardness of life. These observations are so evident and irrefutable that no novel ideas ever rose to challenge them. Equality, as understood by our age, would have been an obscene suggestion.

Of course men are not equal. Each boy who is born into the world is like a seed planted in the ground that has germinated. The seeds grow into saplings and then plants. But there is no guarantee that all will be equally healthy and valuable. For seeds carry within themselves irresistible characteristics. Some good, some bad. Proper tending will help the bad ones to some extent, but the good ones who require less attention will always enjoy a certain pride of place. A boy also comes into the world infused with certain traits. Some of these traits will benefit the tribe, and some will harm. It is the purpose of his people to nurture the good and mitigate the bad.

Such also is the case in the animal world. The stronger, braver buck wins the favor of the female, and one species of animal lords it over another. Even so, some boys will excel their peers in terms of physical and mental capabilities, as well as character. The tribe takes all this into consideration and sorts their men into appropriate channels. To each his part, for the security and happiness of the tribe. To suggest any other ordering of society would have appeared as folly and been met with censure.

Clark opens his eyes when he hears the old man speak again. "Now spread yourselves apart, arm's distance. The men of the village will stand in front of you and test you. No matter what they do, you must not show fear. You must be steady and unmoved. Men!"

At this the men began filtering into the pen. Most carry weapons in their hands or slung over their shoulders. Others, more ominously, carry leather pouches, some of which writhed of their own accord.

"I wonder if Gunthari will be paired with me," Clark wonders, but soon another grownup assumes his place in front of him. Clark has not seen this man before. He has jet black locks tied in voluminous bundles over his shoulders by twine. His arms are stained by ash, as if he had recently been tending a fire. Around his wrists are bracelets of some unknown fabric, with bands of colors: black, then cream, then light blue. His hands are calloused, as were all the men's of the village, and his feet are shod like Gunthari's with one large leather piece folded up and over the toes and sides of the foot. He stands looking into the boy's eyes. Clark breathes deliberately and composes himself, sustaining himself as best he can upon the foundation he has erected in his heart.

"I must not twitch or otherwise show any outward sign of fear."

Clark speaks inwardly, subjugating any rogue inclinations that might seek to unman him and embarrass him. He returns the fierce man's gaze with as much steadiness as he can muster, always checking any urge to appear impudent. There is a brief moment of silence after the men have situated themselves and the group of boys and grownups have spaced themselves sufficiently. The quiet is broken by the old man's instruction, "Begin!" At once activity breaks out across the field. Men begin lunging at the boys with knives and spears, throwing punches that just miss or graze the boys' faces, reaching into sacks and producing serpents or other lizards and taunting the boys, testing their balance by shoving them, or just coming face to face and uttering terrible threats of what they will do to the boy or of how unworthy they think the boy is. Throughout this examination, the boys must not react with anything except perfect equanimity and courage.

Clark finds himself facing down a small club wielded by his tormentor. It is about the length of a man's arm from elbow to fingertips, swathed in white cloth, with a black tip coated in a rubbery looking substance, perhaps pitch. The only words the man speaks to Clark are, "Don't move." As he begins delivering near-misses that come close enough to his head to touch his hair, sometimes from the side, sometimes from above, sometimes straight thrusts, Clark holds to his purpose. He appeals to the pillar of strength within composed of kin and new-found love and faces his trial. He even discovers to his satisfaction that he enjoys it to a degree, his being able to demonstrate courage publicly as he never has before. The sensation he feels is different from his confrontation with the bison in the cave in Spain. Then, he had to overcome a dread that was more primal, more internal. Here in the village, being tested by a man with a club, his apprehension is of a more mundane type, though still serious.

After several simulated attacks, the man quickly changes weapons. He drops the club and clenches his fists and drops into a boxer's stance. Now he begins delivering jabs and right-crosses that graze Clark's nose, cheeks, forehead, and chin. All the while Clark maintains himself stoical, looking inward, jaw set, eyes stern, looking ever forward. He seeks even to control his blinking whenever a blow approaches. He remembers to breathe too, when he realizes his light-headedness is caused by involuntarily holding his breath. *Heed the call.* The words become for Clark a sacred mantra just as the image of his beloved takes on the quality of a talisman in his mind, imparting clarity and encouragement.

Clark is dimly aware of sights and sounds beyond his immediate environs. There are sounds of exertion and grunting, of loud, obnoxious taunts and slurs. Barking dogs are heard also, adding their raucousness to the din. Some men hold serpents entwined about their hands and arms which they taunt the boys with. Clark is vaguely aware of boys who briefly lose their footing before quickly regaining it. "I WON'T lose my footing!" Clark hisses inwardly to himself, issuing as stern an imperative of self-command as he is able.

Now Clark's trainer deftly drops down to the satchel he had placed on the ground and removes something Clark cannot immediately descry. He does not try to follow the man's activity with his gaze, preferring to keep his eyes affixed straight ahead, as if anchoring himself visually. When the man reappears again fully in Clark's frame of vision, his hands hold something that the boy cannot immediately identify. It appears at first glance to be an indefinable motley of dark and light fur, claws, teeth, and stripped wood jutting out at irregular angles. After a time, with greater scrutiny, Clark classifies the imposing object as some species of beaver or mole that has been preserved by taxidermic means and affixed to a wooden shaft. The man smiles leeringly, pleased with his function as official tormentor, and circles to Clark's back, occasionally plunging the furry dead scavenger and making hissing noises. At first Clark finds this facet of the day's training silly, even humorous, but with repeated thrusts and feints of the weirdly stiff animal, including occasional landings on the crown of Clark's head, the boy begins to fight a sensation of combined repulsion and growing irritation with the trial. He feels belittled more than intimidated, and an angry heat starts welling up in his torso. He senses his fists balling up, and uncurls them lest his gesture be taken as an insolent challenge. The man has noticed, and his eyes widen in mock wonder. "Oh, is he getting angry? Is the little boy getting angry? Hmm. I wonder what he'll do next…" At this the man takes the short staff with its impaled animal in both hands and whirls it towards Clark's temple, in an attempt to make him flinch. The essay fails in its intended objective, but instead heightens Clark's already elevated indignation. His still unformed and youthful ideas of self-respect and honor commence to war in his mind, assaulting his will with reproach.

"Am I expected to just take this? This man is disrespecting me. The others are watching. This is no longer a case of withstanding fear, but tolerating dishonor. Why must I endure this? What is the correct protocol? If I push back somehow, I might fail the overall test. But what if I am supposed to, since this oaf has gone off the prescribed course and seeks to bully and mock me? What if SHE is watching?" This last thought sweeps away all doubts and settles his determination. His eyes, which hitherto had remained staring straight and resolute, now turn deliberately and with a studied malice into the face of the man. Clark's ire-darkened jowls and flaring nostrils meet the man's gaze, who for a moment shows surprise but then hardens his own features to match those of the boy. "Looking for trouble, little one? Make your move." Clark braces himself to do just that, and there is a palpable quivering in the atmosphere immediately surrounding the pair.

Just then the old man's voice is heard above the general noise and the blood rushing in Clark's ears. "Stop!" The trial has ended and there is a relaxation throughout the field as men put down their various instruments of torment and boys breathe easy as bodies ease. But not so with one pair. The two are still locked in a contest of will. Clark will not lower his gaze and the man's features become redder and more menacing at this naked impudence. The man closes the distance and moves chest to chest with the young visitor from another world. Clark is afraid, but also proud, and he does not waver. The man is saying something that the boy does not hear because his senses are overwhelmed. All he knows at that moment is that if the man strikes him in any way he will strike back. Both know it and await the clash when the village elder's voice is heard again, insistent this time, and directed at them. "Warin!" The man disengages himself slowly from Clark as he hears his name. Clark resists the urge to wink at him as the man moves away, surprised at his own capacity for cheekiness.

As Clark slowly returns to a state of normalcy, he briefly looks about him. His neck creaks after being held stiffly for so long. As he looks to his right, just outside of the cordons that partition the dusty pitch, he sees her. She is looking at him steadily, with a look he cannot decipher. Is it concern on her face? Reproof? He cannot endure to think this last. He briefly looks into her face without smiling, his features obdurate. His state is too high at the moment, his cheeks on fire and his legs wobbly from the excess of passion. He turns away to look towards the small dais where the old man is speaking.

"Good. Now stop and consider how you performed. If you were

frightened, do not be frightened again. Learn to recognize fear in your body and counter it. Use your failures as guides to understanding and mastering yourself. A man must be a rock, unmoved by the storm raging around him. Be men and serve your people.

"Now take water and rest until you are called. The next trial begins soon."

Clark listens as his chest heaves and trails of sweat course down his forehead. It is hot in the sun, and his excited emotions have raised his body heat. He walks out of the arena in a press of boys and begins looking for a place to refresh himself. He hears his name. "Clark." He looks to his left. Gunthari is standing there beckoning him. He walks towards him, looking him in the eye. The man continues peering into the boy's eyes, assessing. When he speaks he asks merely, "Well?"

"It was…intense."

"Yes, it is meant to be. Did you take anything from it?"

"I need to control myself better."

"We all do. It is a daily warfare we wage against our weaknesses. You did well."

"Gunthari, was he supposed to mock me like that?"

"You don't like being mocked?"

"Of course not. And if I'm training to be a man, and men are not supposed to tolerate disrespect, I thought maybe I should have done something to that…" he catches himself before uttering an oath.

Gunthari smiles broadly, perfectly familiar with the boy's feelings. "It is understandable for you to feel as you do. In fact, it would be odd if you did not feel the sting of your man's honor when it is violated. But remember, it was only a trial, and you are a boy still. You are expected to endure patiently and quietly. Warin did get a bit carried away, though. I will mention it to him.

"What you went through is just a taste of what our boys go through. You won't be here long enough to experience the full training. That would take years. But Alistair wanted me to expose you to our trials to give you an idea, so that is what I aim to do. To give you a taste."

"What parts am I going to miss?"

"The part where the boys leave the village and live out in the wild. They are gone for a month. They have to hunt to survive, and learn to deal with the forces of nature. The gods look after them, as long as they honor them. The boys guard our village from attack by sensing dangers before they arrive at our door. At times they raid other people.

"They will take on the identity and behavior of wolves. Since young men are lusty and ready to fight, this allows them a release. They will wear the skins of wolves and hunt like wolves. They pick a leader of their pack and submit to his authority, like wolves do. They become vicious, animal-like, but this is also a part of their training. Men must be hard when it is time for hardness, and this time in the wild teaches them toughness."

Clark's eyes have grown wide during Gunthari's description. He sees himself joining a troop of boys, leaving comforts behind him, getting rid of softness and replacing it with firmness. He sees himself at night, around a slowly dying fire, looking up at a moon so brightly silver it almost hurts the eyes, and sharing life lessons with other boys his own age. The idea attracts him and his heart yearns for it. "Will I ever be part of a brotherhood?" he wonders, and craves fellowship.

"Are you ready for the next session?"

Clark would rather sit and rest and ponder several things, but he simply says, "Yes."

"Let us go."

Chapter Three

Gunthari leads Clark outside the village, towards a thicket of shade-producing trees close to a stream of cold, fast-flowing water. The other boys are heading there too. The shady area is a welcome sight to Clark. The ground gently slopes towards the bank of the stream, which is narrow enough to be crossed by eight strides. A few tree limbs, made smooth from the activity of the water, lie horizontally across the flow.

"Now you will train with weapons. You will be my partner, since you have not done this before."

Gunthari and Clark walk to a table laden with axes, long knives, and clubs. Some of the handles are wrapped in well-worn, dark brown leather, others are bare. The implements show a good deal of wear, being profusely chipped and dulled. There are also heavy articles of clothing that look like vests, padded with leather and metal studs. Gunthari selects a hatchet and a long blade and two vests. Gunthari motions Clark to wear his vest and Gunthari does the same. He taps Clark on the bicep, "This way." The two select a spot close by the water as pairs of boys position themselves around them. The small grove is now fully populated by armed duos facing one another. The lesson is apparently one that has been practiced before, as there is no need to issue instructions. There is some animated discussion aroused by the armaments, boys being what they are. But the hubbub dies down as usual when the elder speaks.

"Space yourselves apart. That's right. Remember, I want disciplined strikes, no tomfoolery. Now, on my signal,…" He then pauses and continues, "Attack!"

The boys methodically begin executing lunges and strikes, each boy alternating as attacker and attacked. The blades are held in the dominant hand, with the weaker hand in support, gripping the dominant forearm. The strikes are aimed at the necks, torsos, and bellies of the opposite boy. The boys do not strike with full force, for the danger of penetrating the protective vests, but hold back. Some of

the men of the village mill about, correcting the form of the students. "Place your feet wider apart, they're too close together." "Lower your hips." "Step in, don't overextend yourself." "Follow through."

Gunthari now begins providing Clark individualized instruction. "Hold the blade like this, across the palm of your hand. Now close your fingers around it. Now place your other hand here, on your forearm. This hand stabilizes your stabbing hand. Now place your feet shoulder width apart, your strong leg in the back. Don't lean forward. Bend slightly at the waist."

Gunthari demonstrates the motions, and Clark intently observes him. "Yes, that's it. No, don't overextend, and move your feet in tandem, like this." The man and boy perform their drills as dozens of pairs around them also engage in their practiced dance of combat. Occasionally the elder will announce a cessation and then commence another drill, such as defending a strike, or executing a feint.

Clark is elated. This is what he has been yearning for. Finally, he thinks, I am on my way to fulfilling my role as a man. All his previous experiences have been significant as well, but they were of a more metaphysical nature. This is more visceral, more satisfying in a way peculiar to the flesh. As he stabs and lunges and deftly steps aside, he gives himself over to the novelty, embracing the warrior culture. Although he is only taking his first baby steps, he feels certain this is the path not only for him, but for any boy who wishes to reach his natural virile potency. "Focus. Concentrate. This is what you wanted." His inner trainer urges him to excel and endure any pain or fatigue.

When the session is over Clark still has his wind, although his breathing is labored and sweat beads fall from his chin. He feels proud. "I've made it to the end. If I stay focused, I can take whatever trials are thrown at me. I was meant for this." With thoughts like these, he and Gunthari place their instruments back upon the table. They walk back towards the village and Gunthari's habitation. Along the way, Clark spots the nameless beauty across the plaza. She is with other girls, at the edge of a building, laughingly discussing some matter. This time she does not see him, and he takes the opportunity of admiring her, after making a quick inspection to make sure no one is noticing the focus of his attention. He does not relish the thought of being teased or ridiculed. Her jet hair spills in tiny arcs around her forehead where it finds release from the strips that bind it. The ache returns, and he muses to himself, "Will I receive training in how to talk to girls?" He is frightened that his awkwardness and nervousness will betray him and repulse her whenever he finally speaks to her. He must think of a strategy.

Back at Gunthari's, man and boy discuss the day's events. Gunthari asks Clark about his impressions and Clark answers candidly. "I enjoyed it, but I'm disappointed I'm only here for a short while and won't be fully trained like the other boys."

"When you return to your world, you can continue training. I'm sure someone has knowledge, even in your diseased time."

"Not your kind of knowledge. Your people live out your education. You use it to survive. In my world people only learn these things as a kind of recreation. I'm afraid I won't reach a high level of skill."

"If you desire it enough, the gods can show you a way. Do not lose heart. A man's will is his most powerful asset. Activate your will, and you will find strength even without instruction."

They drink water out of wooden cups as they speak. Clark rests his tired body as he sits. He feels accomplished, at least for the day. He reflects that, even though he enjoys book learning and the exercise of his intellect, he is perplexed as to why his world ignores the physical. Sure, there are physical education classes, but even those take place inside of climate-controlled buildings. There is no substitute for being out of doors. Then again, in his world, this is not usually an option, as the untamed outdoors are normally far away from where people live. "I must make time to get into the woods when I return. I'll ask my father to take us camping more often. I'll learn how to survive, how to make use of trees and plants, how to hunt and clean animals. I've never craved these things as much as I do now, but being around Gunthari's tribe makes me appreciate it more. I'm seeing up close a society that lives in oneness with the natural world, and it makes sense to me. I see that without this wisdom of the natural world, no one is fully human. The artificial society I was born into does not satisfy this part of the soul. Instead, it makes us unnatural and unhappy."

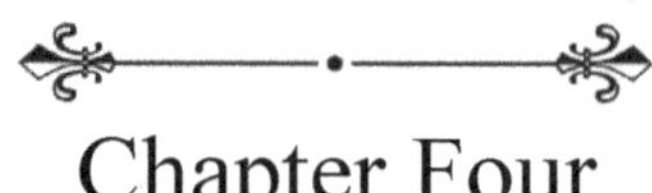

Chapter Four

Over the next several weeks, the boy from our society receives further instruction, and he attends to his lessons with a studied concentration. Clark's awareness of his limited time among Gunthari's folk pricks him to lend greater focus and attention. He endures without complaining, considering silent endurance as part of his learning without being told. He receives further instruction in blade-work as well as spear warfare. He learns how to tie several kinds of knots and how to fasten various items to objects such as trees. He supplements his science of dendrology and herbage when he roamed about with Alistair with new insights. He learns which plant leaves reduce the swelling caused by a wound received in battle, which roots give relief for insomnia, which trees produce resin that can be used as adhesive, and many other uses. He learns to recognize the movements and sounds of birds with regard to enemy activity in an area. He skins and cleans the carcasses of small game like rabbits, as well as fowl. He is not as revolted by blood and entrails as he might have suspected, and this comforts him. "Maybe my true self is emerging."

A day comes when Gunthari informs him to pack supplies for a few days, as the two of them will be spending time in the wild. Clark eagerly anticipates this trip, and imagines all the skills he will acquire when out in the forest. The two hike out early one morning. The sun is just cresting over the mountains when they depart, and it has climbed halfway to its zenith when they arrive. Clark quietly admires the slowly changing topography, as the duo trek into denser and more variegated terrain. Trees grow thicker, and occasionally he spots a gradual slope that leads to a hidden tributary. An occasional large stone the size of livestock interrupts the wood and greenery, casting a queer spell over Clark. "I have to make time and visit those gray stones one day," he muses.

When they reach a clearing near a gently rolling stream Gunthari stops. "Here," is all he says. He surveys the area briefly, then drops his leather pouch and begins preparing the campsite. Clark silently follows his lead. The two set up shelters using tarps as well as dead leaves and branches. After camp is set up, Gunthari asks Clark if he knows how to start a fire. Clark is embarrassed to admit no. Without comment, Gunthari proceeds to offer a tutorial. First he has Clark dig a shallow hole about the length of a forearm. Then he instructs him to gather stones from the stream and arrange them around the hole in a circle. He then shows Clark two methods of ignition, one using a bow, another using a straight stick. Clark struggles to light a blaze, but is finally rewarded after much perspiration and frustration. He carefully introduces the blazing ember into the pile of kindling made from dry leaves and bark shavings. He blows, and within seconds a proper flame is born. He stares at it, mouth open, delighting in his first romance with fire.

Their time in the woodland is attended by lessons in hunting and the repair of tools. The two track deer and wild boar. Gunthari sends Clark to locate small game like badgers in order to increase his familiarity with the dwellers of the forest. He is told not to hunt them, simply to observe. Clark enjoys this, as he is taken with the thought of finding his own way and relying on his instincts. He climbs a few trees and remains very still, allowing the sounds of the animals to announce their presence. He then scans the forest floor, sometimes seeing a disturbance in the underbrush, sometimes sensing it. In this fashion he encounters a pair of beavers commencing their river work as well as a badger out looking for sustenance.

There is also a nighttime foray into the woods. Gunthari tells Clark to rest before sundown, because the two will spend the night in motion. As they wait for nightfall, Gunthari and Clark discuss various matters, with Gunthari doing most of the talking and Clark listening. Occasionally Clark ventures a question, when the timing seems right. He has discovered that the less he talks, the more weight his words carry when he finally does talk. Gunthari speaks of his people and their history, their gods, their ways. He speaks of their conflicts with other tribes as well as alliances made. He tells Clark of the memory preserved by his people of their arrival from the East, and how they wandered over mountains and rivers before finding this wooded land. Here they stopped to build their new lives when the gods gave the sign. Here they displaced the former inhabitants and their softer, gentler gods. Gunthari tells Clark of the hierarchy of the gods, of the All-Father, and the thunder god, and the earth goddess, and of the many other divinities who, from their invisible realm, hold sway over human affairs as well as over natural processes.

Finally, when the sun's light has faded and a cool gentle wind arrives, the two set out. Gunthari tells Clark to allow himself to awaken to the sounds of the forest and to "feel" with his whole being. After some awkwardness, Clark begins to develop his night sense. The whirring of insects and the falling of acorns are magnified. Dark shapes which Clark knows to be trees and clusters of trees give rise to an ominous fear, which Clark endeavors to subjugate. He also beats back the recurring apprehension that some savage claw out of the darkness will suddenly strike him. "Keep it together," he chastises himself. He follows Gunthari without allowing the man to get too far ahead but avoiding following too closely, and thus giving evidence of his nervousness. The walk seems to last long, but this is only a trick of the night. During the day, the same march would not have been remarkable.

After an indeterminate amount of time, the two stop by a clearing on high ground. They had gradually been gaining elevation, and now Clark dimly sees a moonlit landscape below. The masses of trees and their undulation over a rising and falling terrain are like the dark waves of a distant ocean frozen in their furrows. "We will sit here. I want you to hear not only with your ears but with your heart." The two sit still and Clark is all attention. He becomes aware of the creak of his joints and tries not to stir, dismayed that he might be generating noise. The hum of insects, the darkness, his fatigue from maintaining a heightened alertness all combine to make him drowsy. He combats sleep as his eyelids grow heavy.

A sound of rustling from Gunthari rouses him. The man reaches into his knapsack and extracts something and hands it to Clark. "Take this." Clark reaches out his hand and feels something soft and pliable. An animal skin. A wolf skin, in fact, once his eyes adjust. The moonlight reveals a silvery pelt of salt and pepper. "Take off your shirt and put it on." Clark obeys. As soon as he slips on the animal skin over his body and it makes contact with his human skin, a revolution takes place in his soul. A feeling both wondrous and alien makes him dizzy, and he has to pause a few heartbeats in order to steady himself. Inside of the boy, primordial abysses of brute wisdom reveal themselves to him. He is no longer himself, not completely. Of a sudden, he feels at one with his surroundings. He is no longer an awkward intruder in a land not his own, but integral, like the green and brown dappled dirt floor of the forest, like the breezes that make the tree limbs tremble, like the clouds that obscure the moon as they float by.

Clark does not remember the next several hours clearly. He only retains snatches of memory, like a long dream partially and poorly recollected. He sees himself ambling on all fours, his head twisting left and right, looking and hearing. He sees himself using his fingertips to circumnavigate a tree trunk, careful not to disturb whatever is on the other side. He sees himself looking up at the wolfish silhouette of Gunthari against the luminescence of the night sky and thinking, "He and I are one. Our blood is one. What he sees I see. What he hears I hear. We breathe as one."

The dark sky was fading to pink when Clark fully came to himself. He and Gunthari were walking along a deer path, heading towards a collection of boulders off to the left when Gunthari spoke the first words Clark remembers hearing since wearing the wolf skins. "Take them off now." The two remove the skins and the man places them back in his knapsack. Clark chooses to continue without his shirt. To wear a manufactured item so soon after his experience seemed wrong.

When the two return to camp, there is a quick eating of a small meal, then Clark collapses into a deep, undisturbed sleep. He dreams of deep green woods and large shadows, and feels a presence close to him.

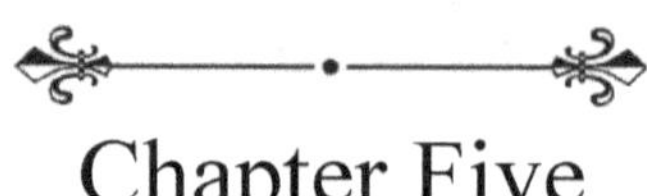

Chapter Five

The two re-enter the village from the same eastward direction they had left. As Clark surveys the villagers going about their daily tasks, he no longer feels the separation of the outlander. Something has happened over night that has drawn him closer to this people. He walks with a new assuredness. In their eyes and in their greetings he perceives an acceptance. Without explanation, a shift has occurred, drawing the boy closer into this world.

As the two approach Gunthari's home, Clark sees her. The boy tells the man that he will meet him later, that he has something to attend to. He is worried that he will be asked questions, but to his relief Gunthari simply says, "Alright then." He seems to understand something.

Over the course of the past several weeks, the boy and girl have caught glimpses of each other and exchanged brief greetings, but nothing beyond this. Clark's attempts at finding her alone have always been frustrated, and the smiles and looks the two have exchanged have only enhanced his fascination. He craves a more concrete meeting. And now, coming out of the forest after a nighttime experience that has elevated his instincts, he spots his chance. The timing seems providential.

Clark conducts a quick mental check. He has washed in the cool stream before breaking camp earlier in the day, so his appearance should not be too dreadful. He passes his fingers through his hair, conducting a hurried coiffure styling. She is walking slowly down a lane, uncustomarily alone. Clark must reach her before she rejoins her friends. He has rehearsed a speech, but jettisons it now. He is still semi-joined to the world of instinct after last night, and wishes to remain obedient to his blood urgings. He trots up to her, and faces her. "Hello."

The girl's eyes open wide at the surprise encounter, and after a pause she answers, "Hello."

"I've been wanting to talk with you. But not here. Let's go somewhere we can talk alone, alright?"

The girl begins to respond, but Clark has already taken her by the hand and led her to a closed off area between two dwellings bordering the edge of the village. He is as taken aback by his unabashedness as she, and he deliberately chooses not to dwell on it lest he break the spell. Her hand is soft and yielding to his touch, and the excitement this elicits in him makes him breathe heavy. Her cheeks are aflame and her breathing also becomes irregular.

Once arrived at a private location, Clark looks into her face. Although he is nervous, he is also alive to a wildness inside him awakened by the evening's activities. He perceives that although potent, this heightened state will not last, and he must act fast before its intensity lessens to nothing. The sight of her scarlet cheeks contrasted with the snowy whiteness of her brow and the dark ringlets idling there make him waver slightly.

"I'm not from your world, but I like it here, and I like you. I've been wanting to talk with you for a long time. I HAVE to talk with you." He pauses, trying not to be carried away by the flood of emotions. This is his first real attempt at approaching a girl.

"Um, my name is Clark."

"Clark," she pronounces with care, unused to the strange name.

"Yes. What's your name?"

"I'm Ava."

"Ava. That's a pretty name. It fits you. It's nice to finally meet you."

"It's nice finally meeting you too."

Ava laughs and looks at her feet when she hears the compliment. When her eyes meet his again they are sparkling and her soft red lips are smiling.

They regard each other, relieved and excited at a meeting that has long been anticipated.

"So, what do you like to do here? I mean, I don't really know your world, but I want to. It's beautiful and fierce, and I'm learning a lot. But I want to learn from you. What does a beautiful girl do here?"

He smiles at her, trying not to dwell on what he is saying but just following the flow wherever it leads him. In a corner of his mind that he has temporarily blocked off, he is astounded and pleased with himself.

"Well, we like to go into the woods, my friends and I, that is, and just explore. We climb rocks, look for hidden grottoes or caves, catch butterflies. Or sometimes we sit still and see if we can see or hear the spirits of the forest.”

“Spirits of the forest?”

“Yes. There are lady spirits who live in the forest. Some say there are seven of them, others say there are more. They dress in white, they sit on large rocks, and they comb their long hair, usually in the sunlight. When you’re walking through the forest and see a shaft of sunlight penetrating through the trees, that’s the best time to look for them. I’m always on the lookout for them.”

“Have you ever seen them?”

Ava exhales dejectedly, “No, not me, not yet, but others have. My friend’s mother, she said when she was a girl, she was playing with her sisters in the house when one of the girls saw something through the window. She asked if anyone was expecting visitors, because she saw a beautiful woman outside dressed in a flowing white gown. The girls went outside to look, and at first didn’t see anything. Then one of them gave a shout and pointed in a direction towards the forest and there, in a beam of golden sunlight, they saw what looked like a woman. She was leaning on her hand like this,” Ava demonstrates, “and her head was tilted back and to the side. The girls just looked at her, amazed, without saying anything. Then she turned her head towards them, and looked as if she was about to say something, but then the sunlight got into the girls’ eyes, and when they could see again, she was gone.”

Clark and Ava remain looking at each other for a few heartbeats, caught up in the thrill of the Otherworld.

“I’d like to help you look for them in the forest, that is, if you don’t mind.”

Ava secretly delights in this idea of the two of them being together in the woods, and she replies, “I don’t mind. I can show you some secret spots where you can hide and watch the squirrels foraging, or a tree we climb to see the forest from above.”

Clark has been fighting an impulse throughout Ava’s talk and he is not sure not whether he ought to act upon it. Calling upon the fading remnants of wolfish instinct still in him, he makes a decision, invokes the wild, leans in and gently kisses Ava on the cheek.

“That sounds like a great idea. I can’t wait for you to show me everything you love about the forest. I want to see it through your eyes.”

Ava’s eyes are still wide and her expression one of astonishment at the kiss. She is simultaneously startled, elated, and confused. Clark is ignorant of all this, or he would try reassuring her somehow.

"Ava, I don't know how often I can see you or when I can see you, but I want you to know that I've been thinking of you a lot, and I'm going to continue thinking of you. I'm going to try and find some time to spend with you. When can I see you? When can we take our walk in the wood?"

"Umm…" Ava tries to find her inner balance after the kiss, "I usually go out with my three closest friends on Wednesdays and Fridays, because that's when we have the fewest chores. If we go out, you can meet us there. Right over there is where we enter the forest." And she points at a spot to the northeast of the village, where a wide road narrows to a thin passage into thick trees.

"I'll try to be there on one of those days, but like I said, it depends on what Gunthari has planned for me.

"Ava, may I kiss you again?"

He asks this as he points at the spot on Ava's left cheek where his lips first touched her skin.

"Mmm…" A hesitation that lasts an eternity for Clark. Ava twists left to right and back again as she mulls it over. Then, too abashed to offer a verbal response, and thoroughly reddened, she nods her head in the affirmative and shuts her eyes tightly. Clark's heart leaps and he kisses her more slowly this time, seeking to savor the union more sweetly than before.

He thanks her then immediately regrets it as a sense of clumsiness assaults him.

"I'll see you as soon as I can." With this, Clark turns away and walks back to Gunthari's residence, as Ava watches him go, elated and brimming with new emotions. It was her first kiss too.

Chapter Six

Gunthari is airing out his knapsack and cleaning his tools when Clark arrives. The warrior has arranged axes and knives and ropes and other implements on the floor and systematically cleans, sharpens, and organizes as needed. The two wolf skins lie next to one another, awaiting their turn. Clark eyes them. Here in the dwelling, away from the context of the forest night, they seem diminished, mere ornamentation, easily overlooked. How strange that objects of such talismanic puissance can revert to the ordinary with a mere change of location and circumstance.

Gunthari is scrubbing the debris of the woods off of his boots with a stiff bristle brush made from the hair of a wild animal just for the purpose as the boy walks in. A gentle shower of pine needles and dust floats onto the floor as the man works his brush around the boots.

"Make sure you clean your gear. A man's gear must always be clean and presentable." He speaks without looking up.

"I'm just going to do that."

Clark makes a spot for himself and seats himself on a small stool. He unslings his own pack and begins laying out its contents.

"That girl's father is Wendelin, a boyhood friend of mine. One of the few left." Gunthari speaks without looking at Clark as he continues cleaning his kit. "It would bring me dishonor if my pupil were to disrespect her in any way."

A flush of indignation roused by the suggestion of impropriety arises now in the boy. He harshly drops what he is doing and looks squarely at Gunthari, who is arranging rope into neat bundles for easy use. "I would NEVER do anything disrespectful towards her." The man continues untangling and cleaning off the tawny rope. "I didn't think so, but it has to be said anyway. I know what is in a boy's heart, because I was one too. And," here he looks up and directly into Clark's face, "you must learn now, as a boy, how to handle women. Handle them as a man, with confidence, and they will respect you. But handle them like a child, and they won't, and you will become frustrated, and you will want to hurt them in your frustration. So in dealing with Ava, or any other woman, I want you to be a man of confidence."

Clark ponders this. It is the most direct lesson he has ever heard about the opposite sex. His parents have always stressed that he should be courteous to all, but they never spoke about girls so bluntly. Maybe one day my father will have this talk with me, Clark thinks. For the time being, it feels good to hear a man like Gunthari speak so authoritatively about such a mystifying subject. Clark has always been adjured to be nice and respectful to girls, and he is. But Gunthari is now suggesting there is a missing ingredient— masculine confidence. Clark had never heard it stated so candidly before. On the contrary, where Clark comes from, society's message to boys is that they needed only to be nice and polite. But here is a man of unassailable virility and manliness asserting a different creed regarding the fairer sex. It catches Clark off guard.

"And how does one become a man of confidence?" he asks, somewhat hesitantly, he realizes to his chagrin.

Gunthari inhales and pauses before responding. "Some men are born that way. But whether he is born that way or not, all men benefit from a strong father who shows them by example. If there is no father, or if he fails in his obligations to his sons, then the boy is at a disadvantage. Still, if he can find a man to pattern his life after, there is hope. But in general, he must make it a habit to believe in himself and follow the truth; to be firm with himself and mature, not childish."

Clark has been listening enraptured. This is the kind of talk he has always wanted to have about life and about the way of men. He has hitherto been unable to find the right someone.

"S-so, about girls," he begins timorously.

"Yes?"

Clark sighs, then: "I want to know some things."

A long talk ensues between boy and man that lasts deep into the night about the mysteries of women.

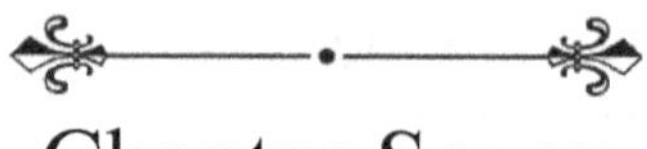

Chapter Seven

Alistair has been researching an area in a remote part of Australia for a possible future assignment when Sophia calls upon him. He is seated at a mahogany desk situated by a window that looks out at an orange-hued, dusty Australian town. He recognizes her advent. She is like a sudden uplifting of the soul and a parting of dark clouds when she approaches.

"How is my Scottish gentleman doing?" she asks exuberantly.

Alistair is a jovial, contented soul by nature, but even his usual state of happiness doubles when the lovely maiden arrives. Today Sophia is wearing a sleeveless black and white top. The collars are wide and brightly white against the inky black of the remaining fabric. Her trousers are gray with a checkered pattern and stylishly form-fitting to her petite frame.

Alistair turns slightly to his right then rises from his dark leather chair to greet his guest with a huge grin born of her arrival.

"Ah, my dear lass, I'm much better now that you're here!" The paunchy man gathers himself up and gaily crosses the floor to receive Sophia in his arms and exchange kisses on the cheek.

His greeting prompts delighted laughter from the girl. "Ha ha! Well, I'm very glad to hear it. And how is the research going? Any prospects for us? Any future students here waiting to meet their future instructor?"

Alistair hooks his thumbs behind the lapels of his slightly rumpled sky-blue blazer as he answers. "I haven't found any solid candidates yet, but I have my hunches, as always." He chuckles, happy to be in converse with his favorite spirit.

Sophia amplifies his merriment by bestowing her youthful smile upon him. "I'm sure you do, and I trust your judgment. Follow your instincts. You have good instincts, my friend." A delicate strand of jet hair on her left temple vibrates like a reed in the wind as she speaks. She rivets her auditor with the sparkle in her dark eyes and their eagerness.

What exactly has Alistair been up to? Well, as you already know dear reader, Sophia is in charge of the selection process of young candidates for the Trials. But she enlists the help of others in identifying possibilities, although the final choice resides with her. Alistair, then, is one member of a larger group of mentors under Sophia's supervision. Clark's selection happened under different circumstances. His light shone so brightly that the maiden herself flew to him, loved him, and assigned him to Alistair. Thus Clark, unbeknownst to him, is of that rarest of rare cases — he was chosen by Sophia herself.

But now Alistair is on the hunt for future adepts. A faint beacon near the center of this southern continent caught his attention and drew him hence. He spends some time "smelling" the air, one might say, until he catches a promising scent. When that happens, he goes to his quarry and makes his observations. The prospect must be of sharp mind, perspicacious, intellectually curious, considerate of others, mature beyond his o her years; an old soul, in brief. The prospect must also be of European descent, as this is Sophia's domain. Other bloodlines are on other trajectories, governed by other invisible colleges.

Today he visited a pretty eleven-year-old blonde girl. Her father works in the cattle ranching industry. She has grown up around animals, dust, and ruggedness. She takes to her environment with a natural inclination passed through generations. Alistair sees her line of descent stretching back to Ireland through the maternal line, and to both Ireland and Germany through the paternal, with a few smaller linkages attached like tributaries. She takes her time before speaking, weighing the conversation and mood first. She observes and listens more than she speaks. This is a good sign. Not all candidates are introspective, but it is more common than extroversion. Introspection lends itself to wonder, and wonder is necessary to soar to the heights made possible by election to the school of the invisible college. Alistair will continue to monitor her.

"Thank you for your confidence, Sophie. It means the *world* ta me. And I hope to come soon to a determination."

"Oh there's no rush! Please, take your time and enjoy the views. This is a beautifully untamed and tough land the children of Europa have established themselves in, and it calls forth the memories in their blood. Stay a while. Who knows, you might find a spot to call home away from home?"

"Ha ha! You'll be hard-pressed to tempt me away from my Scottish homeland, but I can always appreciate a holiday. Ha ha!

"Aye, Australia is a rough, precious stone that stimulates the children, although mechanization has blunted some of its properties, as happens. Still, there are enough children who have been *roused* by this continent's stimulating force. We are sure to find some prospects yet, in spite of *opposing* forces."

At the word "opposing," Alistair's brows furrow, and he looks intently into Sophia's eyes. For the briefest span, her own usually bright visage darkens, but quickly restores itself. "Yes, Alistair, we know about them, of course, but we shall remain above the darkness, agreed? Good. Now, what about our boy Clark? I think he is nearing the end of his initial phase and will need your guidance to make his next transition. He's been a quick study and a pleasure to deal with, Gunthari tells me."

"I'm *delighted* with your pick, Sophie, delighted. I miss the boy and I look forward to hearing all about his Trials. That's always one of my favorite parts, their excitement in relating what they endured! Ha ha! Always brings back memories of my own adventures." The man smiles widely as his fleshy cheeks stretch. His hair, usually obscured by the flat cap, is now free to revel in its disarray of wispy dark and white strands, being indoors.

Sophia, always eager to join in the happiness of others, laughs along with Alistair.

Alistair goes back to his desk and seats himself. Among the several notepads and pens and pencils scattered on the brown desk top protector, there is a familiar book. The Scotsman picks up the black leather bound volume of <u>The Light of Western Civilization</u> and opens to chapter five, *The First Fruits of the West: Greece*. He begins rereading the section so he may have its contents fresh in his mind when he discusses this new phase with Clark.

With the cultural seeds of the Indo-Europeans spread throughout the continent, it remained only for Time to tender its care. Underneath the soil of European cultural life there was an unseen activity, as the newcomers gradually adjusted and sent down their roots into their new earth. A subterranean dynamic energy vibrated throughout. From Ireland to the Balkans, from Lapland to Malta, an event was imminent: the germination of the first green shoot of a high culture civilization. But where would it first manifest? Where would it first penetrate the dark soil of unlettered darkness and silence? To an observer who lives across aeons, it might have seemed a pregnant pause after the noisy intrusion of the Indo-Europeans.

Before answering that question, it would serve us well to learn how the various tribes of Indo-Europeans resolved themselves and where they settled. Broadly speaking, four identifiable groupings arose, all inter-connected, yet distinct. The Celts spread throughout the west, the Germanic peoples claimed the center, the southern coasts were established by the Mediterranean peoples, and the Slavs occupied the east. So it remains today. Of course, this is only a superficial sketch, and does not take into account several smaller groups that do not neatly fit into one of the above classifications, such as the Alpine communities.

So would the first shoot rise up in the Iberian Peninsula, where the Celts had merged with the local population? Or in the heartland between the Rhine and the Elbe, distributed between several tribes of fierce Germans? Or somewhere in the east, in some valley of the Carpathian Mountains where Slavic ways had begun to take root?

In the event, it happened in the southwest, in a most unlikely region: the rocky, rugged, uninviting cluster of islands and mainland known to us as Greece.

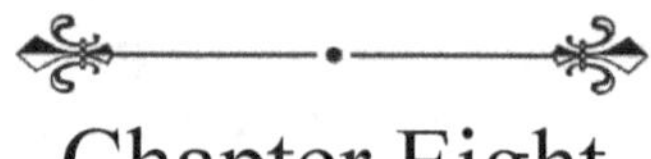

Chapter Eight

Clark awakes feeling invigorated the morning after his discussion with Gunthari and his meeting with Ava. As he rises from his cot to wash up and prepare for breakfast, his step is lively and his mood buoyant.

"Good morning Gunthari," he merrily greets his host.

"Good morning Clark." This is the first time the man has addressed Clark by his name. It makes the boy feel good, and adds to his contentedness.

"What do I have to look forward to today?" Clark asks, uncharacteristically chipper in his inquisitiveness.

"To say your farewells."

Clark does not immediately comprehend what Gunthari is saying.

"My farewells?"

"You are leaving, young one. Alistair contacted me last evening. You will meet with our elders in the afternoon then I will escort you to the spot I found you."

Clark's heart plummets. He has kept this eventuality tucked away from his awareness, unwilling to consider it and hoping it would resolve itself somehow. *I must eventually leave Ava.* He had dared not let the thought take definite form prior to this announcement by Gunthari. Now here it was, staring at him like a steep mountain pass that must be negotiated before continuing a long, uncertain journey. It must be addressed. And like a man.

"You are quiet."

"I think you know what I'm thinking, Gunthari."

"Yes. And I think you already understand what you must do."

"I do. But, may I ask something?"

"Yes."

Clark pauses to collect his thoughts. What exactly does he want to ask? He seeks to probe into a mystery that he probably ought not. But he must know.

"Gunthari, you once were a boy like me, as you said. You know what I'm feeling now. It is a pain like I've never felt before. So can you tell me: Can I see her again? You and Alistair and the rest of you who live in this strange world seem to exist outside of time, so there has to be a way. Is there? If not, how do I overcome what I am feeling?"

Clark has never spoken words of such sincerity and plaintiveness. He kept his voice steady, and he registers this a slight victory against the heart-ruin he now suffers.

Gunthari has listened thoughtfully. His blue eyes catch the light and illuminate like small turquoise caverns as he stands, taking in his ward's address. He wears a dusky tunic, laced in front by leather thongs.

"To answer your first question, anything is possible, but even more so for a man of noble character, so be a man of noble character always. In regard to your second question, separation is a part of life. Your separation from her will be the first of many. Family and friends will die, and your heart will break many times. Learn now to deal with the pain of loss. Let her last memory of you be that of a strong man who knew how to deal with pain. You have to be strong for her."

*   *   *

Clark finds Ava after a search whose frenzy he tried in vain to conceal from others. With parched mouth and shallow breathing, he espies her talking with two friends. As he approaches, he summons his resources and controls the storm raging inside as best he can.

"Hi girls."

She is walking with her friends down a lane that leads to the creek where Clark underwent his weapons training. The girls, unaccustomed to the foreign voice addressing one of their number, stop suddenly and turn around in wonder. Upon seeing him, a look passes between them, and the two friends smile at Ava, who promptly blushes.

"Hello Clark. Clark, these are my good friends, Odilia and Jördis."

"Hello."

They exchange greetings amid excited titters. Clark allows himself temporarily to forget his errand and to enjoy the sweet company of three pretty maids. Odilia is the tallest of the trio. She has light brown hair that is almost red and which is tied in a braid that spills over her right shoulder. Wisps of hair have escaped their captivity around her

87

crown and she arranges her hair now unselfconsciously. She had been running to investigate a rotting log which led to her dishevelment. Light freckles adorn her face, and a thin vein in her forehead now pulsates. Jördis is Ava's height and as golden-blonde as Ava is raven-haired. Her hair is of such yellow vibrancy that it glows in sunlight, as if her blondeness were a gift from the sun. Her serene light blue eyes examine the boy and a faint smile signals her approval. The girls wear white gowns that reach just above their ankles and tunics of red, green, and blue. Taken together, the three are like messengers of nature announcing a jubilee of youth and beauty.

After telling Clark about their morning and the stroll in the woods after finishing chores, Odilia and Jördis exchange glances and take their leave.

"It was nice meeting you Clark," they exclaim. "We hope to see you again so you can tell us stories of your world."

"I would really like that too." Clark's voice now betrays the sorrow that he has kept at bay. The agony of leaving behind a society so akin to his inner longings that it seems tailor made for him threatens to embitter him. Is this some sort of punishment meted out by a stern universe? Ava catches the change in his demeanor and her countenance darkens somewhat. Her smile fades as she looks back to make sure her friends are beyond the range of hearing.

"Clark, what's wrong?"

Clark inhales and composes himself before commencing. "Ava, you know that I am traveling from world to world and that I cannot stay here. I just didn't know it was going to happen this fast."

"What? You're leaving?" Ava's brow wrinkles in alarm and her mouth falls slightly open.

Gunthari's words are in Clark's mind now. *You have to be strong for her.* He swallows hard. "Yes. Today."

He lets the words hang in the air. Ava turns away. She crosses her arms across her torso. She needs to focus on something in order to steady herself. She gazes at a pile of sticks left by a group of boys at play yesterday. "Oh…" is all she can manage for now.

"I don't want to. I want to stay with you. This is the hardest thing I've had to do. But there's still a chance. A chance I can see you again."

Ava's eyes are still riveted on the sticks. "How?"

"I'm not sure, it's a strange process I don't understand, but I will do everything I can to get back here, to get back to you. But," here he pauses and forces the words he does not want to utter, "if I can't, we must both endure. Wherever I am, I will be thinking of you and wishing you happiness. So be happy and be blessed for me, Ava."

The bones and muscles of her neck strain and Clark can't help but absorb this as well as every other detail. His senses are all alive with a painful acuity. Every sight and sound is augmented by the intensity of this hateful farewell. He gently kisses the left cheek that faces him as she continues to stare to her right. This act loosens the tears that Ava has been fighting to contain. Her face contorts into anguish and a flood of tears race down her cheeks and onto the earth. She sobs and shakes.

Clark takes her in his arms. Ava remains with her arms crossed, frozen and unable to move, not even to return Clark's embrace. He just holds her and holds her as she sobs.

He whispers his final words in her ear which rests next to his lips. "Wherever I am, I will carry you in my heart." One last lingering kiss, and he releases his hold against every one of his instincts. He turns and begins walking away. This unfreezes Ava, who now shrieks his name as she races to him. Clark immediately turns and catches her in his arms. "Oh Ava, Ava."

"Clark," is all she can muster. Her face is tear-streaked and scarlet. Suddenly an inspiration occurs to her. She digs into a pocket with the energy of passion and takes out a small object. Clark looks down and sees a bracelet made of colorful rocks strewn along a dark brown leather strip. "Take this. Remember me by it. I made it when I was a little girl. Maybe one day you can give it back to me." And now she kisses him back, her hands behind his neck, lips pressed to his.

The following hours pass like a fog for Clark. He meets with the elder whom he met upon arriving at his house and speaks at some length about the warrior mindset. Clark offers his thanks for being permitted into the life of the tribe and benefitting from their knowledge. His face is stony and his movements made languid by the stupefying impact of his recent heartbreak. The men in the elder's house interpret this as a sign of a growing maturity and seriousness in the youngster. Only Gunthari knows the real reason.

After leaving the dwelling, Gunthari takes Clark aside.

"You spoke with her?"

"Yes."

"You explained the situation to her clearly and plainly?"

"Yes."

"Good. There is one more thing to do now. You must get rid of this surliness. It is not like a man to punish those around him with his anguish just because he is upset. If you can do that, you will go a long way in mastering your heart with regard to girls. Either way, you must stop pouting. It is womanish and un-warriorlike."

Clark knows these words to be true, yet his jaw remains clenched. He resolves to soften his features and master himself by the time they reach their destination.

Gunthari is leading them into the woods towards the east. Clark soon realizes they are walking in the direction from which they entered the village several weeks ago. They walk among the white trunks of slender birches and the sturdy massive columns of oaks. The sun beams begin their struggle to reach the floor as the forest thickens. Clark tries to invite the spirit of the woods inside of him as a salve for his hurts, but mostly fails.

The path is over mostly level ground, with a few undulations. After rising over one of these, and after picking up his head from his chest, Clark sees a figure standing off in the distance next to a beech tree. As he looks, he recognizes the gray flat cap, the tufts of hair escaping their confinement, the coat, and the paunchy form. In spite of his pain, his heart warms. "Alistair!" he thinks, and smiles.

As the duo approach the Scotsman, Alistair's grin becomes visible. His joy at seeing the two of them is sincere and he must express it. He is the first to speak. "Good morning my fine lads!" The older man's mirth erupts in a raspy exultation.

"Good morning Alistair. I hope we didn't keep you waiting long," Gunthari responds. The two clasp hands.

"Not at all, not at all. Besides, how can I complain when surrounded by such beauty?" He waves a strong, aged hand indicating the surrounding woodsy majesty. "And Clark! How good to see you again my boy!"

Clark's face has lost its hardness, his former agony subsumed for now at the reappearance of his original tutor. He smiles with genuine warmth. "Hello Alistair. It's really good to see you too." He extends his hand and grips the man's hand firmly and assuredly. His first impulse is to hug Alistair, but he overrides that impulse for reasons unclear to him. Maybe it would be too childlike, after the weeks of hardening he has undergone? Instead he strives to transfer the intimacy of an embrace into a handshake as best he can.

The two men exchange news of their respective worlds and happenings, Alistair ebullient as always, Gunthari stoic but amiable. The older man gestures with his hands and arms as he tells the Indo-European about his travels in various climes and conditions, the warrior slightly nodding at times, his blue eyes gleaming as they take in and gather information for calculation. "And as always," Alistair ends, "Sophie bids me express her best wishes to you and your kin."

"Pass on my thanks and appreciation to the Maid."

Finally Alistair turns to Clark and says, "Well my fine young man, I think it's time we let Gunthari get back to his affairs, what do you say?"

Clark looks in Gunthari's face hoping to find a support in the wind-tossed landscape that his soul has become in the last several hours. He does in fact find it when he meets the man's steady, penetrating azure gaze.

"Gunthari, sir, thank you. I will always value and remember what you did for me here. All of it."

Here the battle-scarred tribesman extends his hand and Clark takes it. Gunthari allots himself the use of an uncommon expression as he smiles at the boy. "Youngling, it has been a pleasure to train such a willing participant. Continue to build on the foundation you have received here, and I trust you will be the man you seek to become. May the gods guide you."

Clark engages all his remaining faculties to prevent himself from becoming emotional. The farewell to Gunthari and all he represents, the reappearance of Alistair, and the separation from Ava, all conspire to unman him. With his breathing shallow, and with a lump in his throat, he nods his head at Gunthari's final words, then turns to Alistair with his eyes starting to brim.

*   *   *

Alistair and Clark chat briefly about Clark's experiences after Gunthari leaves. Alistair is conscious of the boy's frame of mind and keeps the talk short. He then reaches into his leather carrying pouch after throwing back the flap and extracts the book.

"Remember her?" he asks Clark jovially. Clark is genuinely delighted to see the large tome and he willingly takes it from the older

91

man's grasp. He eagerly flips through its pages and relishes this other reunion.

"I think you know what comes next."

"Chapter Five?"

"That's right. Open to it and let's have a gander."

Clark flips to the start of the chapter.

Book Three

We are composite creatures, made up of soul and body, mind and spirit. When men's attention is fixed upon one to the disregard of the others, human beings result who are only partially developed, their eyes blinded to half of what life offers and the great world holds. But in that antique world of Egypt and the early Asiatic civilizations, that world where the pendulum was swinging ever farther and farther away from all fact, something completely new happened. The Greeks came into being and the world, as we know it, began... Thus in Greece the mind and spirit met on equal terms.

— Edith Hamilton, <u>The Greek Way</u>

Chapter One

Alcibiades of Athens was one of the most flamboyant, most audacious, most brilliant, and most beautiful men ever born to that queen of Greek city-states. Perhaps that is why he was chosen to navigate Clark through the Greek centuries. The two have become great chums, and are now laughing and enjoying red wine in silver goblets, an act of corruption that the playfully mischievous Alcibiades secretly delights in. Let's listen in on their merriment.

Clark, doubled over in laughter and slamming his open palms on the table, responds to his mentor's latest narrative by exclaiming, "Are you KIDDING me?" His face red with mirth and tears streaming, he can barely get the words out.

"I'm SERIOUS!" the former general exclaims, also chuckling and wide-eyed. "He was so startled that he jumped right up like something bit him and started yelling like a girl and running into the woods. People stared with their mouths open like this, and pointed, and, and…" he pauses, laughs, gulps air, then continues, "every time he stepped on a rock or a sharp stick he screamed some more and jumped like this." The Athenian acts out the scene, to the howling amusement of Clark.

His chestnut brown hair cascades lightly on his shoulders in healthy, flowing strands that tremble when he speaks. Eyes of hazel green scrutinize one with a ready alertness and a hint of playful malice. His sensual, medium lips seem always poised to render either a smile or smirk, depending on one's interpretation and disposition. Concave jowls add a natural shadow to his features, and a perfect, smooth, chiseled chin completes the picture of exquisite, good-looking mischievousness.

Alcibiades had been recounting a story of a prank played upon a young man who made the mistake of falling asleep at a drinking party given at Alcibiades' house. When the others noticed, the host gathered the revelers and hatched a scheme. They extinguished the torches and lit some dead leaves on fire, filling the room with smoke. They then tied some bells to the sleeping man's tunic and cleared the way to the door that led outside to ease his escape. An alarum was to be raised and several partygoers were to react with mock consternation to fuel the frenzy. When all was ready, Alcibiades himself let out a raucous and shrill cry of Fire! and a general cry went up from the conspirators. The result was a thoroughly stunned partygoer who finally crashed into a thorny bush to the screeching hilarity from the rest.

The two have spent the night thus, drinking, talking, and laughing, the Greek nobleman serving up story after story to an eager audience of one.

Thus have the pair spent many evenings after days spent in training, traveling, and learning. For Clark has been apprenticed to Alcibiades as a kind of page to a storied knight, and his education has assumed the same character of high adventure and spiritedness that made the Athenian champion both esteemed and notorious.

Now Clark recovers from his fit and prods the Athenian for more anecdotes. The boy has found an eager raconteur of swashbuckle. "Were all your parties like that? Didn't the neighbors complain?"

"My neighbors? I made sure to invite them and they loved my parties! They would be the last ones to complain. There was one fellow though, a grumpy older man. He once made a comment about how out of control my soirees were. I should have just let it go, but I couldn't. So one day, when my friends and I were plotting some mischief or the other, I mentioned his name. They dared me to go punch him! At first I put up a bit of resistance, but I gave in eventually. I walked up to him and whacked him hard." Alcibiades throws a punch in the air to demonstrate. "He just looked at me, stunned. I walked away and laughed a bit with my friends about it. They had been watching from a distance. But I felt bad about it. People were talking about what a scoundrel I was, and they were right of course. Next day I presented myself to him and tore my tunic off. Stripped down naked. I said, 'Here, beat me as much as you like for the disrespect I have shown you. I deserve it.'"

"Whoa! And did he?"

"No. We became good friends though, and he ended up giving me his daughter in marriage, my beloved Hipparete. Gloriously beautiful girl, she was."

The mention of this lovely daughter of Hipponicus, the aggrieved man in the story, suddenly calls to Clark's mind his own beautiful girl. He has tried for several weeks now to blunt the pain of separation from Ava by various means. He tried at times by brute force to will the thoughts away, in keeping with Gunthari's injunction to be strong. This method was mostly unsuccessful. It was a new kind of pain, and his inexperience worked against his attempts to manage it. He would cry at night in his luxurious white linen bed in a plush room decorated with marbled blue walls provided by Alcibiades. His fingertips would gingerly touch the bracelet Ava had given him. He had wanted to keep the tale to himself and nurse his pain until it became bearable, but the combination of Alcibiades' character and the taking of wine at dinner, eventually delivered him of this burden. Clark reasoned that a man of Alcibiades' wide experience and worldliness might be just the right man to confide in and thus alleviate at least some of the heartache.

Thus, Clark found himself recounting his tale. Hesitant at first, he ultimately felt relief. Alcibiades, upon learning of the boy's love-lorn condition, instantly offered advice. "Life is not our friend, Clark, when it comes to matters of the heart or in any other case. Life wants to break us. But consider this as a trial you must pass. Yes, look upon it as an athletic contest. Did I ever tell you I won first place at the Olympics where I raced my horses? No? Well, anyway, it's a good story and I'll have to tell you later. But, returning to you, yes, think of these mini-devastations as competitions for a laurel crown. All men are called to compete in this contest of heartache, so you might as well outdo them. All of us are dealt blows, not only in matters of the heart but in questions of honor, and bodily hurts, and financial ruin. Your goal should be to outdo other men, to bear the pains nobly, like a well-trained boxer who endures knocks that others cannot. This is the real test of manhood — not how many women you have bedded or how tough you are or how wealthy you are — but to withstand the blows of life undaunted. And of course," he raises his silver goblet, "there's always this too!" He clinks his vessel to Clark's and takes a deep draught of the ruby-red liquid.

That evening's talk soothed some of Clark's hurt, though it would continue living within him for a long time. And somewhere in eternity, Ava weeps for her sandy-haired boy.

Chapter Two

The story of the Greeks begins not in the Balkan peninsula but north of the Danube River. For it was from this direction that the ancestors of the civilization known to the world as the "ancient Greeks" proceeded. A convergence of Germanic tribes, themselves descended from Indo-Europeans, began a trek from their northern forest lands southward towards the cobalt blue waters of the Aegean Sea. Included in their number were some who were distant kin of Gunthari and his people.

The journey of these northerners, of what compelled them to leave, and of what they endured on the way to their new homeland, were revealed to Clark beginning several weeks ago via the same method we used to view Sophia's body of students with their tutors. A large, rectangular shaped window made of the sheerest glass or some other mysterious material spread itself out like a cinema screen. Its flatness is so absolute it suggests comparison with the surface of a still pond on a windless, cloudy morning, or with a spillage of mercury on a hard gray smooth floor, so perfectly level and uniform does it spread itself out.

The screen appears on command whenever bidden by a member of the invisible college. And so it was that on Clark's third day after his arrival, and in the country house of Alcibiades outside of Athens, he is invited to sit on a comfortable sofa of firm, cream colored upholstery. The legs and trim are of polished brass that gleam with the sunlight that streams in from windows spilling over with potted plants. Footrests of the same fabric as the sofa cushions support the feet of the duo. A small table with glass top supported on a delicate base of light maple wood rests in front of them. The legs curve sharply outward, matching the shape of the sofa's legs. On the table is an earthen pitcher. It is dyed with rough, hazy horizontal strokes of light blue and faded red. Two simple cups of the same design also rest on the table.

"Today you drink water, so your mind will not be foggy for the lesson." Alcibiades pours Clark water and himself wine. He rests one leg on the table and the other on top of his thigh. He raises his voice slightly and issues a command in the direction of the wall facing them. It is a mostly bare, eggshell white, plastered wall, except for two small framed paintings of still life. Suddenly, on Alcibiades' utterance of "screen!" the aforementioned display emerges from the ether. It fades into view, like a mist that suddenly arises and assumes solid form. It merely shimmers now, like a heavy blanket of liquid silver suspended by an invisible line, but as Alcibiades begins his narration, we see images appear that illustrate his tale.

"This will be a lesson about the origins of my people, Clark, they who are known to you as 'the Greeks.' It's a strange thing, these labels we use to identify people. Every kindred has a story, a story of where they came from and how they came to be. And those stories always involve a transformation, a transformation from one kind of people into another. So let us sit back and behold the transformation of several groups of kin who became the Greeks of history."

As Alcibiades finishes his sentence, the screen comes alive with movement. A disturbance on the surface like heavy ripples of water quickly resolves itself into a view of Greece seen from far above. The bony fingers of the southern peninsula stretch their brown digits into an Aegean Sea pocked with wispy clouds. To the north, across the Ionian Sea which separates the Peloponnese from the mainland, patches of green in Thessaly and near Mount Olympus add color to the mostly dun topography. As Clark looks, small vibrating points and clusters of points of light begin glistening all over the land in various groupings. Clark recognizes the lights from his vision on the bridge with Alistair. He knows, then, that they represent people. The golden lights are of varied hues and brightness. Some are golden-brown, others reddish-brown, others yet different gradations of gold.

"The lights represent the many folks who swarmed over this rugged land for millennia speaking a motley of tongues that eventually rendered the classical Greek that I speak. Let's meet some of the leading characters in this pageant, shall we?

"First, I shall briefly describe the multiple inhabitants of early Greece whose only major contribution to future generations was their dizzying pantheon of gods. We called these forerunners of our race the Pelasgians, which doesn't really do anyone any justice as it is only a generic term. We use it to lump them together. Suffice to say, they were the indigenous dwellers, or, as indigenous as we are going to get, because these lands have been inhabited for an exceedingly long time."

As the Athenian speaks, an assortment of lights vibrate and glisten at a noticeably higher frequency than the others in order to indicate the Pelasgians. "Many of these so-called Pelasgians are descended from those who lived here before the Indo-Europeans. They spoke languages now unknown, faded away out of memory. We do not so much as know what they called themselves. But they left behind an assortment of gods, goddesses, and demigods that we later incorporated into our own systems of belief. For the old gods never really die or leave, but they undergo transformation as well." As he speaks, ghostly images appear, superimposed over the Greek homeland. Clark is confused by them at first, until he realizes he is looking at deities left behind from that older Greece. Alcibiades provides commentary. "This one with the wings of an owl became the goddess Athena. She was fully a bird at one point, then assumed human form over time. Oh, and that one there…" And so the conversation went on, until all the older gods were identified and described.

Afterwards Clark asks, "And what about Zeus?"

"Zeus was brought into Greece by the Indo-Europeans. He was blended to fit the older gods, along with the other deities brought in by the newcomers from the north. And speaking of the newcomers…" Now a patchwork of lights on the screen begins marching southward down the Balkan peninsula and into the Greek mainland. As they spread, the screen is illuminated throughout mainland Greece, especially near the Isthmus of Corinth, where one light outshines the rest. "You are looking at the Mycenean civilization. They were the first flowering of the Indo-Europeans on Greek soil. By the time they built, or occupied, their first palaces, such as there, at Mycenae," Alcibiades indicates the brightest glowing point, "most of Greek culture as you know it had taken form. Gods, goddesses, customs, and language had blended like a stew of several ingredients, until a new culture had arisen — we Greeks! Or rather, we Hellenes, as we refer to ourselves. And what a people we are. Or were. Or… you get my meaning." He laughs, then becomes quiet for a few moments, then, "It was truly an honor to have been born a Greek." Alcibiades raises his cup in salute, then thoughtfully takes a slow drink of his wine.

The pair then discuss the earlier Minoan culture that flourished on

Crete and which inspired Mycenean culture until eventually taken over by them. Alcibiades mentions in rapid succession the many smaller tribes and clans who occupied Greece, both on the mainland and on the islands, and eventually on the coastlines of foreign lands where colonists had migrated.

Alcibiades pauses. "That is a lot of information to absorb. What do you think so far?"

Clark's brow furrows. "It looks like a tangled mess."

"Oh it is, it is," Alcibiades laughs. "But you will find this same confusion of languages, customs, and blood ties repeated throughout Europa, but perhaps not as frustratingly as in the case of the Greeks."

They talk of the sudden collapse of the Myceneans and the dark ages that followed. The screen keeps pace with him, as the lights flicker and then diminish at the close of the Mycenean era. "It was during this period of instability and historical darkness that the most Greek of all Greek poets composed his song of the bygone age. For during the Mycenean period a war had been fought between themselves and an enemy to the east, the Trojans. And it was Homer who took upon himself the retelling of that glorious struggle between Greek and non-Greek. His poetry is like hearing the blood of our people transformed into music."

An armor clad warrior with reddish-blonde hair suddenly appears, clutching a spear and looking towards them with a ferocious visage that is as menacing as he is handsome. His long hair is bound in the back and rises with healthy volume above his bronze brow. His eyes are light blue, almost gray. His legs are shod with shining greaves tied with leather straps and buckled in the back. He seems ready to bound into the room where the two sit.

"Achilles?" Clark conjectures.

Alcibiades smiles. "Aye, Achilles. Just look at him! The splendor of this magnificent beast." The two admire this superb example of warriorhood, Clark with wide eyes, Alcibiades with a thin approving smile.

"Many a youth tried to conform his life to the template provided by this king of the Myrmidons. Arrogant and selfish he was, yes, to be sure, but these qualities were overlooked in one who shone so brightly, like a shooting star, in his battlefield exploits. It was his example that fired the imagination of a young Macedonian king who one day conquered the world. Or, at least, the parts worth conquering."

A parade of images dances across the screen, and Clark is transfixed by the spectacle of ships with bright, billowing sails embroidered with colorful designs; with armies composed of hard-looking men, some noticeably larger than others, many of them ruggedly fetching in their military attire; with the fair, Greek wives who tearfully bid farewell to their gallants on the eve of departure for Troy; of the crash of man on man in the teeth-clenching slog of combat, bodies shoving, blades looking for soft targets. Clark barely draws breath. The sights and sounds excite a heart that has been whetted by its recent experiences in the Black Forest for just this sort of martial struggle. He wants to leap into the screen and strap on a breastplate and lunge at enemies with spear in hand.

After the conflict ends and as black smoke plumes above a Troy that has been reduced to rubble, Clark relaxes the tension that has gripped him during the scenes of battle. He does not speak. The screen shimmers slightly as it returns to its original overhead view of the Hellenic landmass and islands.

"Moving stuff, isn't it? Now you have some insight into the Greek heart." Alcibiades raises his cup towards Clark and the two toast a glory that has echoed down the millennia. "To Hellas!" They drink and exhale with satisfaction.

Chapter Three

Alcibiades stands up, places his earthen cup on the glass top, adjusts his clothing, turns to Clark and says, "Right, that's enough for now. I don't want to overwhelm you with an excess of information or you will tire of Greece, and I want you to love her!"

Clark rises as well, still holding his cup. "I doubt I could ever tire of Greece. I was mesmerized the whole time. This was always one of my favorite cultures to study, and now that I'm learning from you, I'm even more fascinated."

Alcibiades grins with genuine satisfaction. "Ha ha! I'm glad to have such an eager pupil. There is still much more to learn and to see. We have only begun our journey through Hellas. You will be moved even further by what awaits us. Glories and triumphs abound in my people's history. But come for now." Alcibiades begins walking through the entranceway that leads to a patio. Clark quaffs the remaining liquid and sets his cup down and follows.

The patio is a small space with a small white table and three white chairs. Blades of grass poke through the brownish-red colored tiles under their feet. Small fruit trees line the walls of the enclosure. Marble statues of wood nymphs lurk throughout the perimeter, stark white against the green grass. Upon the table are two weapons of a kind Clark has not seen before. Alcibiades picks one up and begins cutting figure eight patterns in the air. "Pick it up," he instructs Clark, who is eyeing the other lustily. Clark does so. He grips the short sword by its meticulously crafted handle of boar's tusk ivory. The pommel and hilt are of polished black onyx. A thrill shoots through the young man upon gripping a weapon of such exquisite design. He delivers a few thrusts and cutting motions learned from his time with Gunthari. Alcibiades offers advice. "Spread your feet a bit apart. Don't lean. Remember to breathe."

As the two execute their slicing and stabbing motions, Alcibiades relates to Clark some personal anecdotes. "I've always loved swordplay. The feel and the look of a sword excite a man's spirit. It is like an external part of our soul, the part that craves adventure and trials." Here he pauses and brings the weapon down by his right side. "It is the sword that became the universal form of belligerent communication throughout the world. But for us Greeks it was secondary. The spear came first. I may show you its use later. The sword was a backup weapon. But where you are going, sword-knowledge will be more valuable for you. The age of the spear will recede the more you travel in the future."

Clark now places his blade back on the table and faces the Athenian. "How was it, Alcibiades? How was combat? I mean, fighting and killing back then, man to man? In my age men shoot from very long distances. To us, sword and spear combat seems unthinkably terrifying."

Alcibiades smooths his white tunic as he speaks. "You must remember, I was born into an era of close combat and constant war, so I never knew anything different. Every boy in Greece, and throughout the rest of the ancient world, anticipated going to war and facing combat. Or, at the very least, defending his property from robbers at a time when police forces were mostly unknown. It was a violent world, so when you finally saw yourself facing an enemy across a field, you were more or less prepared for the butchery that was to follow. But it was still terrifying, and no doubt about it.

"Me personally, I took it in stride. I reasoned with myself, 'I am a man, and a man's function is to fight and kill at times. I accept this ordinance from the gods.' That was enough for me. It helped me overcome the shock and revulsion that might otherwise have crippled me. The sad truth is," Alcibiades chuckles, "I rather liked it. It was like the highest form of athletic competition, and I always had a competitive spirit. So I looked forward to it, as to a foot race or a boxing match. It helped to calm the nerves somewhat. For me at least. But then again, I was a bit of a scoundrel, so perhaps I'm not the best example!" He smiles his wry smile.

Clark ponders this. He will return to these thoughts later. His boy's mind has been awakened to the possibility of violence, and found both dread and excitement in its contemplation.

In the weeks that follow, Alcibiades adds to Clark's martial education begun by Gunthari. The two practice with sword and with shield. Clark learns how to strap on the shield and grip it tightly, curling his fingers around the leather-coated grip. He learns how to use it both defensively and offensively. The combination of sword in right hand and shield in left combined with footwork always transports the young man to realms of soldierly enchantment. "This feels GOOD! This is where I belong. This is right." Thoughts such as these churn in his mind. Whenever he feels the sweat beads forming on his brow, his ardor intensifies. Clark has not been a part of any serious, organized athletic team, except for intramurals at his school. Thus the training he has undergone in his recent travels serve as his first foray into the field of hard physical instruction. Clark welcomes the sweat and pounding chest and the following day's soreness as part of his initiation into the community of manhood. He thirsts to become a man, to be seen by others as a man, to be respected as a man. All boys want this, but Clark's vision of manhood is touched by something grander. He wants both the fighting prowess of the warrior and the gallantry of the knight. A fusion of Achilles and Galahad would be best, in his estimation. He holds the image in his mind like a sculptor sees a statue in a block of marble, still unwrought, waiting to be liberated by the chisel. Vaguely, as through a haze, he sees himself a grown man, standing on a height with sword in hand, bronze skin glistening, sinews rippling, steady eye beholding his domain. And thus, as his lessons continue, Clark strives to add muscle and tissue to the ethereal.

Chapter Four

Along with Clark's physical training, there are places to visit and people to meet. Alcibiades takes him on a tour of Hellenic civilization much as a museum tour guide leads a group, except in this museum, the exhibits are real places and historical figures. But before walking among the olive groves and the agoras of the Greeks, Alcibiades reveals to his young dependent the older world which preceded them and which nurtured them in their cultural infancy.

One day, not long after Clark's arrival, the two walk into a circular, darkened room with marble floor. On the hard white marble is a star-shaped design. The star radiates out its spokes in several directions from a thick center, touching the limit of the marble. The dark bluish-green of the star is bordered by a gold band. Dimly, Clark sees small, column-shaped tables with busts or vases along the perimeter of the chamber. "This room will serve as our theater of the mind, Clark, for the things I want to show you deserve to be experienced fully and luxuriously.

"No culture develops in a vacuum. There are always antecedents. Greece is no different. Not to take away anything from the Greeks and their extraordinary development, but in fairness and honesty, we shall briefly touch upon the ancients who established the older world and served as a foundation to us Hellenes."

As he speaks, the walls of the circular room first darken to black, then begin to lighten with images that encircle the pair. They are now standing amidst a reddish desert with sand drifts. In the distance, bright, colorful buildings emerge and soon draw nearer, as if the two were being drawn towards them in a chariot. Clark soon identifies familiar figures among the edifices, as jackal-headed statues and seated pharaohs come into view. "We're in Egypt."

"Yes, Egypt, one of two mother civilizations, it could be said. Where this extraordinary people emerged, we never knew. They seemed to arise from the sand, or perhaps from the green flood plains of the Nile. But whatever their origin, they loomed large over the area and inspired others with their way of life, as a torch that enkindles tinder. You saw, when we reviewed the Minoan and Mycenean civilizations, the clear examples of Egyptian influence."

"Yes, I remember. The gigantic stone temples, the serious-looking statues. It looked like it was made by Egyptians, or, anyway, that was my first impression."

"And you were correct, in a way. For Egyptian arts and sciences found themselves replicated by the neighboring nations who were awed by such a towering cultural achievement. So overpowering was the Egyptian influence, that it was almost necessary to sunder oneself from it in order to make something new. And that is what eventually happened in Greece."

As before, with the screen, Alcibiades' words evoke the images that now surround them in the projection chamber. Clark sees cyclopean walls of temples. He sees Egyptian surgeons performing complex operations upon patients drugged into painless stupor. He glimpses Egyptian architects sketching blueprints on thin parchment and discussing the merits of various types of materials needed to support the weight of an arch or sustain dyes in the hot sun. And of course there are the pyramids. Clark marvels as them, matched against the blue sky. He has heard that they had once been decorated with several colors, but nothing prepared him for the sight of the pyramids in their original glory. Enormous, smooth masses of blinding white, of light-absorbing black, of cool green, arise from the sands like the building blocks of a tribe of giant children. Clark becomes slightly dizzy with the beholding of so much splendor.

"Magnificent race, aren't they? To raise up from an unforgiving desert land so much majesty. It's no wonder the stamp of Egyptian culture can be seen in so many areas within their influence. They loomed large over the simpler races of the eastern Mediterranean. If any were to evolve in another direction, it was necessary to detach from the awesome influence of the Nile civilization and find one's own path."

Now the images that wrapped around them slowly metamorphosed into a different landscape. Here was also an unforgiving desert land, blasted by a severe sun. But the hue of the sand and the contours of the land made it clear they were no longer surveying Egypt.

"Now we move further to the east, deep into the very heart of the oldest of the old. In a land we Greeks called 'the land between the rivers,' or Mesopotamia, we find the first significant blossoming of the human race."

Now Clark sees a collection of herders and pastoralists tending their animals and living a hard life of subsistence. Then Clark sees them moving through time in a quick fashion, collecting around a central area, discussing plans for building and organizing. Slowly at first, then more quickly, he sees settlements arising near the two great rivers of the Tigris and the Euphrates. He sees more clans of hunters and herders moving towards the new cluster of villages. Then the villages solidify into cities, the first cities. Crude habitations make way for more substantial buildings of oven-baked bricks. Straight, well-planned streets emerge, and walls suddenly arise forming protective boundaries. All this takes place within the space of about fifteen heartbeats. Now Clark beholds an organized landscape of irrigated fields, sturdy city walls, plazas, gardens, terraces of blue and gold with billowing curtains, and a mighty ochre ziggurat dominating the entire scene. The citizens have substituted their rough pastoral garb for refined attire, the product of a mingling of textile technology brought to the cities by divers artisans. For thus did this foundational civilization will itself out of the silence of ages, by the combined intelligences of sundry people. They were summoned to this hub of human development like moths to a blaze. Once mobilized, the inevitable process of social development occurred, awaiting its own arrival like seeds which contain the promise of a forest.

"The Sumerians. This is as far back as we need go, Clark. For the Greeks drew inspiration from no older societies than these eastern peoples between the great rivers. The Sumerians lit a spark that raged far and wide. Using their achievement as a stepping-stone, later cultures arose, as well as the first empires: the Akkadians, the Babylonians, the Persians, and the many lesser nations which, taken together, compose a tapestry of humanity."

Clark has been gazing at the panoramas unfolding before him with unmitigated delight and wonder. The contrast with European woodlands with their greenery and wetness heightens his curiosity. The glimpses of vast, arid regions streaked with life-bestowing rivers bordered by lushness offers a vivid comparison. The sight of palm tree orchards gently swaying in hot winds and of languid river commerce flowing up and down reed-lined waterways beguile Clark's memory for a long time afterwards.

Gradually, the images darken to black, leaving only the white marble floor visible. Then the margins of the room come into view again. Clark stands inert, in a state of awe that is swiftly developing into a normalcy. Every vision of a vanished culture he is allotted by his mentors stirs him and adds contours to his increasing weltanschauung.

"Hungry?" Alcibiades inquires cavalierly. "Uh, yeah," Clark stammers, still in the throes of his latest astonishment. "Excellent. I'm famished. Let's have lunch." And off the Greek strides out of the diminutive, circular structure in the direction of the house.

Chapter Five

Dear reader, you might be wondering what Clark's travels and experiences are leading to, or what purpose they serve apart from supplying him with a sense of personal fulfillment. Well, in the interest of honesty, and hopefully of keeping your attention, here is the totality of meaning of Clark's instruction.

As was mentioned at the beginning of this tale, the West is sick and dying. All mighty civilizations undergo an ebb and flow of vitality, and often for the same reason: to wit, they neglect the primal impulses that exalted them and thus slacken into a dangerous laxity. This laxity results from too much luxury and excess. A people thus enervated commence a gradual slide into corruption, like clean, clear water sluiced away from a healthy stream into a murky bog. They begin experimenting with novelties in their ennui in order to while away the time, and opening doors that are better left closed. So it goes with the West today.

Clark, from a young age, manifested in himself those characteristics that promote the health and restoration of his fallen people. From the time he could reason, he craved Beauty and Order. Ugliness and Chaos disgusted him, though he could not articulate precisely why. The reason should be clearer to you now, reader. The West, like all cultures, has a way of healing itself. By a process of seemingly blind selection, a few boys and girls are born infused with the choicest virtues of a given bloodline or bloodlines. By just such a method, Clark was selected to be a member of the school of the hidden society.

We have compared him to a blossom of unusual beauty, carefully chosen by an ever watchful gardener. Let us add another comparison. He is a spark in a dark place, a gleaming beacon for a lost throng groping in a shadowy territory. Sophia saw this spark and sped down to enliven it. His spark must be tended lest it be extinguished through neglect, blown out and left smoldering by a callous, indifferent wind. If he remains true to his noble nature, if he *heeds the call*, there is hope. He will return to his people a hero bearing a boon won after a fabulous journey.

Thus I beg your indulgence, gentle reader, as we follow our young man in his quest for manhood. For, although he is not fully aware of it yet, his transformation is not for himself alone. He is a soldier in a loosely organized army fighting against the legions of decay and ruin. May he prosper!

Chapter Six

Clark usually begins the day by reading in his book. This time he has kept it, Alistair having handed it over to him. It rests upon a slim round table with a shiny, round marble top streaked with black veins supported by a black, fluted column resting on a rounded base of black, frilly lace design. He keeps it closed in order to protect the spine from cracking. The table is next to his bed and he likes keeping the book near him like a charm when he sleeps. Now he picks it up and walks it over to the desk located across from the foot of his bed. The desk is made of mirrors. Mirror top, mirrors for cabinets, mirrors along the sides. All mirrors. He places the black volume upon this bright surface and opens it with cautious fingers, flipping pages with care. He turns to the chapter that transported him here when he last saw Alistair: chapter five, the Greek chapter.

After arriving in this shady suburb of ancient Athens, and after Alistair introduced him to Alcibiades, the book was temporarily forgotten. There is always such a commotion of activity and a delight of the senses awaiting him at his new destinations, that all other considerations are put aside. But now that he has time to himself, after acclimation, he turns to the origin of all his present wonderment.

"I will treasure this book for all my days. One day, when I live in a big, comfortable house with a fireplace and a personal library lined with leather-bound books, this book will enjoy a special place. I'll have a craftsman build a custom-made lectern connected to the wall where I'll rest it. A permanent light will glow on it, like a special exhibit at a museum. Or, will constant light damage it? I'll have to do research on it. Anyway, it'll enjoy an honored position, I can tell you that much."

Musing thusly, Clark admires the full-page plate that adorns the start of the fifth chapter. Every chapter begins thus with an imposing graphic that gleams on the glossy pages. Not too glossy, just enough to imbue the pages with a certain opulence while avoiding garishness. The image is an artist's representation of the goddess Athena. She stands upon a dark field of battle with warriors' bodies strewn about in the background. One warrior bleeds from a spear thrust in his side. He struggles to cling to life, to ward off death for one more day. He rests one arm on the earth and inclines the other towards the goddess shimmering in her white peplos draped over her military armor. She is tall, as tall as the tallest male fighter in any campaign. She stares out coldly from the page at the viewer, her lips thin and severe, her eyes cheerless, her chin level. None of the dead and dying warrant her attention. She favors only the champions left standing at the end of a conflict and cannot be bothered with beseeching pawns. The sky is a hazy, smoke-clogged pink, as night descends over a terrain cluttered with the dying and their whimperings of "mother! mother!" the dead with their stupid faces, and broken military matériel. There is no mercy is the painting, only the austere elegance of Necessity.

Clark stays riveted on the picture, his eyes ravenously taking in every dark detail. The image raises questions he hadn't fully considered. What is the purpose of it all? Is yearning for glory and prestige accursed? Is masculine culture right, wrong, or somewhere in between? And the question most urgently provoked by the sight of a beautiful, stern goddess radiant in her power: are the gods real?

Chapter Seven

“Are the gods real?” Clark asks Alcibiades one day, catching him off guard.

The two had been discussing the responsibility a man owes his country and countrymen when these are under attack. The lesson had begun when Alcibiades asked Clark, “Under what circumstances, if any, should a man lay down his life?” This question led to a lively talk which was supplemented by a visit with from Alcibiades’ former teacher, Socrates.

The old philosopher and his pupil embrace amid smiles and laughter. The younger Athenian then introduces his own student, Clark, to the stout, pugnacious thinker. “Clark, meet the man who once saved my life in combat!” Socrates responds to this eulogy with a gentle shove on Alcibiades’ shoulder and a shushing. “Oh my boy, will you quit repeating that line! It was no more than you would have done for me, and more ably too, seeing how I tripped once or twice and stepped on you!” This memory incites more levity from the pair and Clark can’t help but be drawn into their warm camaraderie.

The old Athenian philosopher has a face that seems carved out of a spoiled eggplant. It is lumpy and unattractive, with a nose that seems like a twisted knot soggy with seawater. Two dark piggish eyes look out from recesses of soft pink flesh, and lips like stuffed earthworms form a grin that is not winsome. His overall aspect is that of a male version of an ugly washerwoman that lives on the edges of society.

When Socrates joins the discussion, he listens patiently to Clark’s responses. He nods his head at Clark’s suggestion that protection of one’s loved ones warrants self-sacrifice. He then asks the boy from our world, “And who are our loved ones?”

“Our family, sir, mainly. And I guess close friends would count too.”

“Yes, very good. I concur. But shall we enlarge the definition of ‘family’ to include those members of society who share our lineage? Those who proceed from the same ancestry and bloodlines? Is it reasonable to conjecture that a man's tribe is an extension of his family?"

"Yes sir, I can agree to that."

"And would it be judicious to apply the same standard of self-sacrifice to this extended family as to that of our immediate kin?"

"I...I'm not sure, sir, but I can see how it might be right to do so."

"I understand your unwillingness to commit to a solid answer, because the issue under question, self-sacrifice, is a serious one, and if justified, must be carefully considered in all its complexity. Let me then take a different approach..."

In this manner, Clark receives his first lesson in the Socratic method from the best source possible.

The talk ranges far and wide, with Socrates comparing families and their peculiar traits with nations and their own corresponding peculiar traits. Just as one can detect similarities between parents, children, grandparents, cousins, aunts, and uncles, so too can one detect similarities between tribes and nations. And just as a family distinguishes itself in athletics or academic excellence, a tribe or nation distinguishes itself by means of special characteristics.

At one point Socrates references the gods in order to add weight to his case. "For the gods have seen fit to organize all life in a systemized way, from animals up to human beings, each according to their kind. There is an order in the world that marks it as the result of intelligence and not blind chance. Thus one perceives family-like connections in the nations of men."

The mention of the gods reminded Clark he wanted to ask Alcibiades about them. Afterwards, when they were alone, Clark asks his question.

Alcibiades stares off for a moment, uncharacteristically quiet. Then, "The gods are...not what you think Clark. I can't discuss them, as I've been asked not to. I'll only say this: think of who the gods favor, according to the myths and stories, and who they ignore. Only the heroes seem to warrant their attention. They are like athletic trainers who care only for the top athletes and treat the rest with contempt. That should make you pause and consider."

"But then, they're REAL? In some way? How can they..."

"I told you I can't explain it further."

Clark's recently acquired taciturn disposition falters at the knowledge that the gods of Greece exist, at least in some fashion. And

Alcibiades' reticence only fuels his curiosity. Clark does not hear the following admonition about refraining from asking more. His ears are pounding and his mind swirls. The gods are real! The thought rarely leaves his mind over the next several days. He resolves to discover more about this enthralling subject through means other than Alcibiades, but he is not sure where to go.

Back in his room he opens his book and eagerly turns to the chapter on Greece. He scans hurriedly, hungrily, looking for any reference to the Olympians. He sees a box of text offset from the main page entitled "Divinities of Greece." He reads,

The Indo-Europeans brought with them members of their native pantheon and later absorbed new deities from the indigenous populations. Thus Zeus and the divine twins Castor and Pollux entered Greece via the invasion, and old gods of Sky and Earth were assimilated. The gods did not remain static. They changed and developed over the centuries. Apollo, for example, originally governed prophecy and healing. He later gained provenance over music and light.

There was no official religious doctrine that bound the various Greeks to one worship; rather, every region had its own traditions. The closest thing to a unifying element were the works of Homer, whose masterpieces, The Iliad and The Odyssey, were universally revered.

Eventually a kind of uniformity resulted after years of evolution. A widely accepted pantheon emerged from the swirling and shuffling of divinities — the Olympian gods. Besides these were a myriad of lesser gods, forest and water spirits, subterranean demon-like beings, and a primordial family whence proceeded all. Each city favored a selection of these immortals and fostered their association with them via temples and religious celebrations.

Clark remains non-plussed afterwards. Interesting information, but it doesn't address my burning question, he thinks. How can they be real?

Then a thought emerges that would better be quashed instead of fostered. Maybe there is a way of contacting them? Clark does not pursue this thought initially, as it seems too far-fetched, but it arises again and again, gnawing at him. He plays with the notion of how such a communication can be effected. Didn't he read once about people burning incense in temples to statues of the gods? Is there a temple nearby he can visit, just to satisfy his curiosity? Nothing more, he tells himself. Just research.

One day he tells Alcibiades that he would like to visit the city center, the agora, in order to experience Athenian life. So the two walk into the city, talking and discussing matters and enjoying the views. It is early summer and there is a bloom upon the earth. From Alcibiades' house they can see the Acropolis looming like a watchman above the city, stern and ever vigilant. When they reach the town center, Alcibiades stops and talks with several citizens, introducing Clark as his protegee. Cups of wine are offered and accepted. Dainties consisting of candied dates and sweet breads are enjoyed by the two. But Clark is slightly distracted by his mission. He remains alert for any sign of sacred activity. When the two pass their first temple, a small edifice dedicated to Artemis, Clark smells incense and sees young, attractive priestesses dressed in flowing gowns of various bright colors attending to their duties. Some are sweeping the floor of marble, some are adjusting the tapestries that were recently hung up for the impending feast, and others are carefully arranging the food and flowers left by pious visitors as offerings to the goddess. Clark takes in as much as he can as he walks by. He espies large, brass bowls as wide as a man is tall with small foot stools beside them. Sweet, aromatic, white smoke billows up from the bowls, spicing the air. The sounds of clucking cocks, barking dogs, and lowing cattle intermingle with the sounds of merchants plying their wares, boys playing in the streets, and horse-drawn carriages ricketing along bumpy roads. All these sights, sounds, and smells dizzy Clark with a welcome euphoria.

As the two finish their delicacies and drain their cups, Clark tries asking Alcibiades as innocently as possible if they can visit a temple. He tries cloaking his intentions by invoking the beauty of the sculptures and that of the priestesses as his prime motivations. He seems to succeed, as Alcibiades reacts with the hoped for mischievous grin.

The two wind their way up to the Parthenon. But this is not the Parthenon of Clark's acquaintance. It is not the structure shattered into a permanent state of disrepair by an explosion in the 17th century that severed the West from a connection to her ancient beauty. No, this is the Parthenon in all its glory. Clark and Alcibiades are walking up the steep pathway to a temple that is only a few decades old. It graces the prominence that is the Acropolis with a radiance that makes Clark fall silent. Its sides and columns reflect an unblemished and radiant white light that cause the eyes to squint. The frieze atop the entrance with its vivid, multicolored bas-relief serves as a stunning counterpoint. A band of people on foot and on horseback process across the frieze in an eternal parade. Below, a similar activity occurs as the faithful go up and down, on their way to offer sacrifice and back down again. They carry pigeons and cocks, as well as sacks of incense. Before they reach the edifice, these faithful arrive at an outer area where priestesses pour libations onto altars and worshippers throw incense on fires tended by temple aides.

The two pass through this throng and the smoke and arrive at the Parthenon. As the pair climb the stairs, a mounting elation grows in Clark. He feels stunned not only by aesthetic arrest but also by the sincere piety of the worshippers. Clark has rarely attended church services, except on family religious holidays like Christmas and Easter, and rarely even then. Religion has never really mattered to him. The past few weeks however have opened channels in his heart. Now this latest assault on his spiritually blasé, American mundaneness further stirs the waters in the well of his soul.

When the two arrive at the top of the stairs, they walk directly to the massive sculpture of the virgin goddess at the far end of the temple, a resplendent, glittering sculpture of gold and ivory. She stands with her weight transferred to her right leg, the left leg is slightly bent. Her left hand rests atop a shield, her right hand holds an image of winged Nike, the embodiment of victory. Discordant sounds of suppliants' voices and the scratching of sandals upon the polished floor echo throughout.

Clark has managed to separate himself from Alcibiades in order to carry out his task. As he stands looking up at the statue, his eyes search hers. They are painted blue and contain no warmth, although they are pretty to behold. An unexpected hesitation now arises in him, though he could not identify its meaning. Some dim warning, perhaps, but he does not pay it much attention. The daylight hour and the stir of activity drive away the faint darkness, and Clark continues his purpose. With his eyes looking up at Athena's, and feeling both slightly silly and unhopeful, he mutters these words: "O goddess, if you are real, I would like to know you. Will you show me some sign?"

After the words are uttered, he senses a kind of efficacy, as if the words have in fact reached their intended target and now await a result. He continues to stand there, anticipating something, not knowing what. After several more moments, he resolves to walk away and rejoin Alcibiades and allow whatever invisible forces there may be to take their course. Instead, he is compelled to take a backward glance. A sound, like the rustling of dry leaves or waves crashing on a wintry shore, seems to whisper his name: "Claaark." He looks but does not see anything.

Chapter Eight

The following day finds the pair back at the garden training area practicing their swordplay again after another lesson via the shiny, glimmering screen. Clark begins thinking of it as the "the quicksilver." He has only recently learned the term in school in science class. The teacher was discussing the properties of mercury and mentioned its alternative name. The name made an impression upon Clark's imagination, and he uses it now to christen his unusual mode of instruction. The day's seminar covered the colonization of various coastlines by the Greeks, some near the mainland, some further away, like Italy and Sicily. Each colony retained some of the savor of the motherland while developing its own distinctive seasoning, as is natural with colonies. And many colonies produced thinkers whose originality added to the Hellenic cultural feast. Alcibiades outlined the lives and teachings of the various scientists and philosophers who sprouted out of this colonial fertility. Pythagoras, Diogenes, Hippocrates, Thales, and a score of others parade before Clark's eyes in a cavalcade of scientific romance. Alcibiades produces objects from a wooden chest painted black and white, to better illuminate the lessons: a glass orb encased in a loose mesh of wooden pegs and rope; a flat, shiny, brass disk with carved markings and thin metallic needles serving as arrows; a heavy, brass cylinder with gears that fits snugly in the palm of the hand.

After the two wrap up their exercises in the garden and store the weapons, Clark goes back to his room for his accustomed afternoon break. Along the way, he looks up at the blossoms of white and pink that decorate the tree branches shot through with golden sunbeams. He focuses on the light breaking through the leaves like bright drops of liquid. Some intimation makes him pause, a feeling of expectation. The memory of yesterday's visit with the statue quickly returns. Could a sign be imminent? His head begins to feel light and there is a buzzing in his temples. His mouth opens in an "O" as a wave of unexplained exhilaration emanates from his chest sending a tingling throughout his body.

"What is about to happen?" Clark ponders as he feels himself lifted on the crest of a new sensation. His normal awareness is swept aside and replaced by a new way of understanding. His usual thoughts cease, and in their place is a noiseless peace. All mundane concerns are swept away by this wave and in their place instead stand an infused confidence and assuredness that do not belong to the boy. He feels enveloped by a joy and a peace he has never known before. He feels that he might walk across a battlefield and emerge unscathed by virtue of this invisible mantle of protection. He turns to look behind him as if to locate the source of this blessing but only sees the stony path that leads back to Alcibiades' place, only now all is more colorful and in sharper contrast than before.

Clark looks about him, and beholds the world as he never had before. There is a softness to everything. There is also a kind of glow suffusing all, and in that glow is serenity and safekeeping. All anxiety has fled, replaced with a tranquility not known since his mother cradled him when he was an infant. Clark is beyond questioning now and allows himself to be a vessel of this cascade of lightness and serenity. He chooses to walk more, and take advantage of this new state. As he walks, everything he sees and hears is transformed into loveliness. His ache for Ava subsides and he can think of her without his accustomed pain. She is still there in his mind, but he glimpses her as through a glass that softens all into a picture of harmony and contentedness. "How much longer will this last?" he wonders, but dismisses the thought, suspecting he might ruin the experience by analyzing it.

And so he spends what might be minutes or hours strolling around the grounds, examining the leaves of trees, and pebbles along the path, and blades of grass, and all manner of details that he normally ignores. All of it, every fiber of the world, now sings to Clark of beauty and rest. He does not know how long he remained in this state, as time lost its meaning for him, but he senses dimly that this cannot endure. We are not meant to dwell in uninterrupted bliss while in this round.

Clark is now back in his room, lying on his bed, looking up at the ceiling of his room. There is a thought he has not allowed to ponder out of a sense of foreboding, but he now indulges it: "Is this from you, goddess?"

From somewhere in his mind the immediate and definitive reply comes, "No."

Clark does not hear it with his ears but with some other faculty. He is momentarily jarred, but soon recovers, and continues his query.

"Then who are *you*?"

"Your protector. You must not attempt to speak to the gods again. They are not gods. They mean you harm."

Clark lies still and ponders this. He tries to understand before asking more. He has learned not to ask too many questions, to arrive at answers with as little bother as possible for those around him. He recollects all he can about the gods and about his interaction with the statue of Athena yesterday. He recalls the callous disregard of the goddess in the picture he saw days ago. He recalls what Alcibiades told him about the nature of the gods and his hesitancy to say more. He recalls that when he thought he heard his name called in the temple there was a hint of menace. But then who bestowed upon him this morning's pure joy?

"Did you create my joy today?" he asks.

"I did this in order to show you that your true allies want your happiness and to teach you there are false allies that want your downfall."

"Are you my ancestors?"

"No, but I was with them as well. Stay on your path. Heed the call."

Clark contemplates this and soon falls into a dreamless slumber.

Chapter Nine

Clark awakens later that afternoon. The same inner calm is still there, but less intense. He slowly remembers. He feels peckish and goes in search of food. As he assembles a plate of cheese, bread, and fruit, he hears Alcibiades calling him.

"I'm in here."

The Athenian walks into the kitchen area and appraises Clark for a moment, as if looking for some sign. Just as Clark is about to ask what is the matter, Alcibiades says, "Bring your plate into the dining room."

Clark follows his mentor. Without saying anything, Alcibiades eases himself into the couch, summons the screen, and calls it into life. Clark sits next to him and eats as he looks at the screen.

"This is why we no longer address the gods. Look."

Clark is paralyzed for a few seconds. How does Alcibiades know? A feeling of embarrassment washes over Clark, as if he has been caught out in a shameful act.

"Oh don't be too distressed, my young friend. At some point they all succumb to the temptations of the forbidden. But I want you to be informed about these things now that you've rolled the dice." He winks at the boy. "Alistair told me. We have to keep a watch over our students. You see there," he points to the screen. Clark sees a series of similar images. In each one, there is a multitude of people either bowing or with outstretched arms. At the front of each multitude are what seem like priests. Some of the people are clearly Egyptians, other Sumerians, but many others are unknown to Clark. Their clothing, the natural environment, and their physical appearance belong to several nations throughout the world. Clark thinks he recognizes Mesoamerican or South American features among them, but can't be sure. In any case, the theme is the same: a great mass of people are engaging in various forms of religious worship orchestrated by a priestly class. There are also statues representing the respective deities. After reviewing many such sacred assemblies, Clark begins to detect something ominous.

"The gods of the various nations are like vampires in a way, Clark. Vampires with their own herds of human cattle to feed upon. What they feed upon is not blood, but worship. Obedience. This is food for them. They maintain a priestly class which in turn maintains a steady supply of sustenance for the gods. The gods then bestow power on the priests in the form of social superiority. Sometimes they endow them with special abilities, cheap parlor tricks to keep the civilians in line. Magic, if you will. The rulers are part of this scheme as well, although often unwillingly."

The perspective changes, and instead of looking down at the masses of peoples, Clark is looking out at them from the point of view of the statues and totems. Clark seems to hear inside his head a sinister groaning, or something like discordant music. He intuits that these sounds emanate from the gods, and in the sounds there is menace. Clark feels in his chest that the deities hold the people in contempt. They long to rip and tear and rend the faithful. That they withhold this urge is owed only to practicality. They must tend to their cattle, propagate them, in order to maintain a steady supply of humans to feed upon. Their disdain, their evil, is so unabashed that Clark feels ill. Some mechanism allows him temporarily to unite with them in order to gain a deeper understanding of their motives. This is part of the lesson, he apprehends, but a very disturbing part. The ill-will of the gods is a constant, churning, maelstrom of seething malevolence. Amid this profound scorn, Clark identifies something else: envy. The gods seemingly envy some aspect of the human condition but Clark cannot quite make out what it is.

Now the quicksilver shows something else. A rocky, rugged terrain. A jagged mountain peak like a knife with a serrated edge that Clark somehow knows to be Mount Olympus. Now he sees various promontories overlooking plains. One of them is the Acropolis in Athens. But there are many others in other cities. He is being shown Greece. But this is a primordial Greece. No marble temples with fluted columns yet rise from the earth. Instead, Clark beholds several mud brick constructions built around sacred springs or groves. He sees simple bronze vessels with burning coals inside and worshippers tossing incense. But something distinguishes these faithful from those of the other nations shown to him. Before he can think about this further, the scene swiftly changes again. Now he sees athletes performing stretches, oiling themselves up and getting ready for a competition. He sees also citizen soldiers performing their military exercises, getting into formations at the trumpet's call, forming shield walls. These then return home after the day's training where their wives have dinner ready. Now the scene switches to an ad hoc assembly of men discussing the affairs of state, whether they ought to ally themselves with a nearby city or remain neutral in an upcoming conflict.

Alcibiades asks Clark, "What is different? What do you notice?"

Clark thinks hard before answering. "I don't see the Greeks worshipping in the same way as the other peoples."

"No, but you know that Greeks did worship gods. But how do you think their worship differed from the non-Greeks? Do you see any signs?"

Again Clark tries to grasp the meaning. "They seem more, I don't know, independent? The other cultures just seemed to go along with the system. But the Greeks look like they take matters into their own hands. And they compete in sports, although I'm not sure how this is related to the gods."

Alcibiades grins. "You are right, Clark. The Greeks ARE different. And this difference was something that thwarted the gods, eventually undermining their influence. For, although many Greeks were sincerely pious, they were simultaneously active, stimulated by an impulse of the blood. This was the result of centuries of conditioning, both by rugged Greece herself, and in their original homelands further to the north. Europa has this effect on all of her children. And the result of this European conditioning was the unique spirit of the West, a spirit that was strong enough to resist total enslavement by the hungry, jealous gods. Do you follow?"

Again Clark must pause in order to weigh this new information. He crinkles his brow and wipes his hair from his eyes. "I think so. Do you mean that because the Greeks are so independent and because they think for themselves, that the gods weren't able to totally dominate them the way they did the others?"

"YES! You've got it. Ha ha! Like I always say, I'm proud to be a member of such a race as mine. It was in Greece where the spark was first lit, the spark that Europa had been trying to ignite for generations. Like a woodsman rubbing a stick onto another stick, tired and frustrated, until he is finally rewarded with smoke and then flame, so it was with us. With the Greeks. The spark of *Logos* erupted among us first, and we set the rest of the continent and world on fire!"

Something about this revelation does not sit right with Clark. He thinks of Gunthari. He honored the gods, and he didn't seem enslaved. He seemed rather to be one of the freest men Clark had ever met. He couldn't square this conundrum so he decides to ask Alcibiades.

"But, do you mean,… Gunthari for example. You know him and what he's like. Is he enslaved by the gods? He didn't seem so to me. Yet he honors the gods of his people."

Alcibiades exhales. "No. Good point. Gunthari is a strong, formidable man and no one's slave. So let me elaborate on the nature of gods and of men.

"Human beings crave union with the divine, with something beyond themselves. This urge is healthy and natural. But there were, and are, invisible powers willing to exploit this human longing. Human beings with strong, clean characters, with honest yearnings, attract to themselves good forces. Those who yield to the depraved, debased part of human nature fall into the traps of the gods. Gunthari and his people are of the strong kind. They value honor and justice. They are not liars. They are self-sufficient. They choose their leaders according to merit, whether they are deemed worthy men, not according to the whims of a priestly class. They do not practice human sacrifice, let alone child sacrifice. Because of this, the false 'gods' are mostly unable to subjugate them."

"You mentioned 'good forces.'"

"Like the ones that chose you, Clark. You manifest in yourself those qualities that attract the good and repel the bad. But your curiosity got the better of you yesterday and an attack was planned on you, an attack that was thwarted by your invisible protectors. That is today's lesson: stay true to your higher nature, and do not be tempted by your lower impulses, those impulses for dark mysteries, for quick solutions and sudden insights. For magic and such. That will open doorways to the so-called gods. Do you know that among the priestly classes of other nations there were always a large contingent of exorcists? Those priests who specialize in the removal of evils spirits? And that among the European peoples this practice was much less widespread? It is because the European spirit is freer, more liberated, more prone to justice and righteousness. It does not typically lust after the craven pleasures that get one possessed by the dark gods."

Clark sits silently. Everything Alcibiades has said leaves him feeling chastened. For Clark knows that he made the decision to address the goddess in the temple against his better judgment. Something gnawed at him that day, counselling him against such an act. But this instinct he ignored. And now he is reaping the consequences. He feels mortified, and does not like it one bit.

But Alcibiades' good cheer is irrepressible, and he soon takes his sapling outside for another round of training. This time it is boxing. The two review footwork and changing levels. Clark trains with a renewed intensity, utterly obedient and silent, as a self-imposed penance for his transgression.

Chapter Ten

"Well that's been sorted. I feel for the youngster. He is hard on himself and will not soon forgive himself for this slip. But he will learn from it. Such is experience, that great teacher."

"Yes, my dear Alistair, his sense of fair play and justice is strong, that is why he is so harsh with himself. And that is what I saw in him from the beginning. He won't do it again I think."

Alistair and Sophia engage in a short conference after recent events. Alistair is a bit tousled looking. His clothes are more disheveled than usual, his breathing a bit labored, although slowly stabilizing. It was he who rose to fight off the chthonic, snarling thing that was making its way for Clark after being summoned by the boy's naivete and curiosity. Such are the unseen activities of the invisible college. Such are the dangers and disturbances that their students are unaware of.

Chapter Eleven

nd so the weeks passed. The boy from our world and the ancient Athenian spent many a day talking, engaged in lessons at the "quicksilver," training in swordplay, wrestling, boxing, and sampling all the delicacies of wine and fodder that Alcibiades can dream up. When we first encountered the pair, Clark was telling Alcibiades about Ava and of his pain. Alcibiades eagerly offered life advice. We now rejoin them there.

Clark goes to bed with a light heart. The wine, the wild anecdotes, the sharing of Clark's sorrow over Ava, all served to ease his mind and prepare him for a comfortable rest. Before retiring, he walks to the table and looks at the book's cover. It has begun to gather some dust which Clark now wipes away with his sleeve. Rather than opening it, he places it squarely in front of him and looks at it. He sits and thinks over the past several weeks, trying to synthesize his experiences into a whole. The story of the Greeks presents a more complex puzzle than Gunthari's Germanic tribe. In the Black Forest, life seemed simpler, easier to grasp, although tougher. There were fewer questions that needed answering and the people followed the instincts conferred upon them by previous generations. How were the Greeks different? Or maybe that was the wrong question, Clark thinks. He puts it to himself another way: At what point in time were the Greeks similar to Gunthari's people, and at what point in time did they diverge? That seems better. For the Hellenes *evolved*. That was what Clark noticed. They did not remain static. The Greeks of the Trojan War were not the Greeks who rewarded playwrights at Athens, or who postulated that the Earth was round using the lengths of shadows, or developed an organized system of geometry. The ruffians had added intellectual grace and elegance to their social milieu.

Clark tries to determine the point in the Greek timeline when the shift happened. The point when this loose affiliation of Mediterranean kinfolk transitioned from a standard Indo-European warrior society into a prodigy of talent and high accomplishments, when they blazed onto the world stage through a display of virtuosity. And what did Alcibiades mean when he said, "the spark of Logos erupted among us first"? He has meant to ask him that.

He opens the book and tries to find an answer. He skims headings and letterboxes. He sees one heading that catches his eye: the Dark Ages. It comes between the age of heroes during the Trojan War and the flowering of Greek civilization. Maybe there is a hint there? Clark reads,

> *The Greece of mythological proportions and the Greece of philosophy is divided by a Dark Age. The ancient Mediterranean world suffered a cultural setback that to this day has not been fully explained. A series of invasions, possibly also natural disasters, retarded the development of much of the eastern half of the great sea. There was both permanent loss and temporary loss. The Hittites would never recover and the so-called New Kingdom of Egypt came to an end. The Greek peninsula and her islands, however, were among the fortunate who rallied from the devastation with fresh vigor. After the Mycenaean megarons were destroyed and lay in ruins, various city-states from the peninsula began a slow ascent out of obscurity into prominence. Athens, Corinth, Thebes, Sparta, and other poleis would take the place of the earlier centers of power. The celebrated Greece of high culture famous throughout the world was finally coming into existence out of the ashes of an earlier, shattered world.*

This was all very interesting, but Clark still cannot identify precisely what were the specific cultural seeds that spawned the rise of "*the celebrated Greece of high culture.*" He gathers his thoughts and organizes them as best he can according to what he has learned over the past several weeks with Alcibiades. Before the Dark Ages, there was a vigorous culture led by a warrior aristocracy that engaged in constant fighting and lived life to the fullest. The arts of war predominated, and ornate weapons such as spears, swords, and shields were esteemed. Wine flowed at banquet halls, and adventurous sea-faring voyages rounded the picture. This was the generation of heroes. These were the names that lived on for ages afterwards, a bottomless cauldron of bubbling inspiration nourishing future generations. Before this Heroic Age came movements of peoples through a series of migrations into the peninsula and surrounding islands that saw a mixing of the newly arrived and the indigenous natives, who had themselves previously migrated from elsewhere. Maybe, thought Clark, Greek exceptionalism is to be found in these earlier periods. But all he can weave from these threads is that the infusion of Indo-European lustihood added the right fuel to the original inhabitants and from this admixture arose the future Greek greatness.

And where were the gods in all of this? He forces himself to think about this, although it causes him to wince. His recent dealings with the shadowy powers has left him a bit out of sorts. But he tries to sweep aside his personal feelings and think objectively. Those gods that urged on their devotees to fight, like fans at an athletic contest, and occasionally interfered in the game itself: where did they go, and what of their influence during and after the Dark Age?

Then it occurs to him that the Greeks who emerged out of the post-Heroic Age were splintered. Whatever unity they had before was mostly gone. Each city was its own political organism with hardly any connection to other cities except culturally. They spoke the same language, with small variations, and worshipped the same gods. They venerated the same poet in the form of Homer, and generally shared a common cultural identity. But these ties did not lead to a concord among them. They strove fiercely with one another, militarily and politically.

And then there were the Olympics. Clark remembers how much the Greeks enjoyed athletic competition and also how this trait distinguished them from other peoples. Every four years competitors from throughout Greece would convene in order to represent their city-state in rivalry with other city-states. Truces were honored and hostilities paused in order to allow for the games. Although Clark sees the Olympics as a kind of proxy for war, he senses there is something else, some conclusion he thinks can be drawn from the Greek spirit of competition that lurks just outside his awareness. As far as he knows, few if any other cultures on Earth at the time engaged in such large scale competitiveness. Naturally other folk played their own sports, but the scope of Greek games was vast, encompassing the whole civilization. Clark wonders about this and what it means when he alights upon a notion: Maybe it was their fierce independence that secured their autonomy? Maybe, reasoned Clark, the enslaving gods were unable fully to govern the Greeks due to their prevailing spirit of ruggedness. The best they could do was to adapt their scheming to the unique character of the Hellenes and thereby gain some form of dominion over them, while never quite overmastering them as they had other peoples.

"What did you mean by Logos the other day, Alcibiades?"

Clark and his current mentor are finishing up their morning calisthenics routine. They spend half an hour doing stretches and resistance exercises.

"Hmm? What?"

"You said that 'Logos' emerged among the Greeks first."

Alcibiades takes a few panting breaths and looks at a spot on the floor before answering. "Yes. 'Logos' is a term used by our philosophers and given many meanings. But over time, it has come to mean something like the 'inner light of reason.' My teacher, Socrates, whom you met, spoke widely about it, although he is not the origin of the concept." He pauses and wipes sweat from his brow. "It meant only 'speech' or 'text' but slowly developed into a more profound, more philosophical term. Anyway, why do you ask?"

"Just trying to understand you Greeks that's all. I mean, why you're different, where it all came from."

The Athenian looks up to regard a passing cloud then blurts, "Ah who knows? Ha ha! The spark had to ignite somewhere."

He playfully slugs Clark on the shoulder and reaches for a towel and wipes his face. He hands one to Clark.

"Let's clean up and have a snack, my precocious protégé. I'll meet you in the dining hall."

And that was that. Clark contemplates Alcibiades' reply as he washes up and changes clothes.

Chapter Twelve

The following weeks followed the same schedule of swordplay and hand to hand combat with lessons at the quicksilver and visits to the town for diversion. And of course Alcibiades' company is a diversion in itself. But the lessons are approaching their end because Greek history is approaching its fin de siècle. Already the two have discussed the Persian menace and the consequent Greek triumph in the Persian Wars followed by the fratricide of the Peloponnesian War. The rise of the Romans in Italia casts a shadow that will soon obscure the Hellenes.

But Clark gleaned much about the Greeks in their glory days. He has taken up the habit of writing his thoughts down in order to organize the growing information. His mentor provided him with writing materials which took some getting used to, as they differed from his custom, but Clark enjoys the look and feel of the ivory stylus in his hand.

He sketches his thoughts and observations after each lesson and as they occur to him. Here are some recent excerpts:

** The Greeks start becoming more aware of justice and philosophy after the Dark Age. There are still kings in most cities, except Athens, but they don't have complete control. They are kept in check by others so they don't get out of hand. And they are warrior kings who fight at the head of their troops in battle.*

** They still honor the old heroes like Achilles and Hercules, and try to live up to those standards, but they are also more civilized too, more into the arts and sciences. They have the best of both worlds then — toughness for battle, and the intelligence and creativity that lead to high culture.*

** The Greeks enjoy things like sports and theatre. They enjoy* *entertainment for the sake of entertainment. They like to compete and to award prizes in competitions. I don't see this happening outside of Greece. It's like a whole different side of the human spirit awoke in the Greeks.*

Clark's mind returns to his discussion with Alcibiades about the Greek independent spirit. The idea had continued to churn in his mind, a nagging that he knew he had to return to. There was some unresolved matter in it that demanded his attention. "So, it seems like the gods' power over the Greeks after the Dark Age became even weaker. The Greeks had become so independent, so free, so in love with play and with life in general, that they were harder to control."

And this idea birthed more hard by: even though the other Indo-Europeans put on competitions and awarded prizes, they were less organized, less systematized. They did not enjoy the geographical intimacy of the Greeks. For the hilly, rugged lands of the Greeks provided just the right proportions of distance and nearness to facilitate travel and cultural intercourse. The Celts, Germans, Iberians, Slavs, and others were hindered by forests, plains, and rivers that hampered a closer association. But the Hellenes proudly strutted upon a promontory that poked into the sea, unenvied and unmolested by neighbors.

And the Greeks were mariners also. They imported and exported. They discovered and colonized. They learned and synthesized. The engine of cultural evolution burned the fuel provided by this exchange of goods and concepts.

"And that's why," thought Clark, "Greece is where the chemical reaction happened, the reaction that had to happen somewhere eventually. The Indo-Europeans were like a bubbling, seething, thick soup of organic matter, like in some scientific lab. Once the conditions were right, something had to happen. And Greece is where this spark first occurred, like Alcibiades said. He called it 'Logos,' but it could be called a chemical reaction too, I guess."

Clark muses further that such a patrimony ought to be esteemed. Such an eruption of human potential has to mean something, it has to have value. And moreover, a period of such surpassing human achievement ought to be studied by future ages in order to keep the fires stoked, those flames of human innovation and progress. Clark reckons it is not a given that people will create and maintain high culture, with all its benefits and blessings. It is too much like a sandcastle built close to the shore, constantly threatened by villainous waves seeking to erode the edifice. Care must be taken and stewardship implemented to keep the structure sound.

He puts away his notes and prepares himself for bed, his head still filled with the thoughts of the day. Maybe tomorrow I will grasp some new insight, he muses.

But tomorrow, Clark will bid farewell to Alcibiades and travel to a new time and place again.

About the Author

Eddie Zapata is an American who discovered European literature at an early age and was smitten for life.

Born and raised in Chicago, he joined the United States Marine Corps, where he served six years. Overseas duty included Somalia, Okinawa, Honduras, and Morocco. He was a schoolteacher for approximately eight total years, mainly at the high school level.

He travels in Europe as often as time and resources allow, and continues his studies in European literature, history, and philosophy.

He currently lives in beautiful Louisville, Colorado, and visits the mountains and the woods as often as possible.